Nucco tried to look away from the eyes that blazed down into his, but he couldn't. They held his sight as a magnet holds a needle. The face above seemed to shimmer before him: that lipless gash of a mouth that scarcely opened when the *Spider* spoke; that predatory beak of a nose.

"What did Dwyer tell you?" the command came now. "Speak!"

Cold, merciless fury was in the *Spider's* voice. This was an old trick of the underworld—to blame any infamous series of crimes on the *Spider*, to brand his name with the origin of the very evil he risked his life to combat.

"What did Dwyer..." he began to repeat and then it happened!

The sudden crash of gunfire filled the room, Nucco's shriek mingling with the harsh reverberations, and in the same instant the *Spider's* hair-trigger reaction had carried him over to the light switch with a bound. The room plunged into darkness.

In 1943, Donald Cormack penned the last SPIDER novel commissioned by the original publisher. Now, for the first time ever, readers can thrill to The Spider's final adventure in print! When law-abiding citizens are marched into death row, society scion Richard Wentworth discerns a plot to destroy city leaders. Follow the Spider into blazing combat when he challeneges the criminal cadre known only as **SLAUGHTER, INC.!**

To learn more about *The Spider*, and his amazing adventures from Moonstone Books, see pages 173 through 176, or read more at

www.moonstonebooks.com

MASTER of MEN!
SPIDER®

SLAUGHTER, INC.

by
Donald Cormack

Introduction by
Will Murray

The Spider: Slaughter, Inc.

Rich Harvey, Editor

Stephen Bryant, cover artwork

Cover Design by
Erik Enervold/Simian Brothers Creative

Interior Book Design by
Rich Harvey/Bold Venture Press

The Spider: Slaughter Incorporated
ISBN: 978-1-936814-21-3

PUBLISHER'S NOTE:

Published by
Moonstone Entertainment, Inc.
582 Torrence Ave.,
Calumet City, IL 60409
www.moonstonebooks.com

This one's for
DONALD CORMACK,
the forgotten
"Grant Stockbridge"

... until now ...

Art: John Fleming Gould

Conducted for the SPIDER
by Will Murray
Internationally known pulp historian and author

S laughter, Inc. is the lost Spider novel, a strange orphan of the fading fortunes of Popular Publications' *Spider* magazine in its final year, 1943.

The *Spider* began his blood-soaked career a decade before, in the deep Depression year of 1933. Popular Publications publisher Henry Steeger saw that Street & Smith was doing a roaring business with their *Shadow Magazine,* based on the famous radio voice and bylined Maxwell Grant. Steeger was frank that he was out to steal away as many *Shadow* readers as he could.

"The reason we started the title *The Spider* was because of the success of Street & Smith's *The Shadow*," he said. "At this point in pulp history, individual titles became very popular, so we decided to try a few ourselves."

In a story similar to Stan Lee's recounting of the origin of Spider-Man, Steeger claimed that a solitary spider walking across a tennis court gave him the inspiration for the creepy character. He hired a famous mystery novelist and occultist, R.T.M. Scott to write

The Spider made his debut with a cover by Doc Savage artist Walter Baumhofer.

The Spider saga ended in 1943 — with a cover by Raphael DeSoto. Moonstone is proud to continue the character's legacy.

the first novel, *The Spider Strikes!* The first issue hit newsstands in September, 1933 cover-dated October. Scott's byline appeared in the second *Spider* story, but to this day there is a mystery over what happened next.

For when the third issue appeared it bore the house name of Grant Stockbridge—a bold attempt to lure Maxwell Grant fans. Behind that concocted byline lurked Virginia-born writer and newspaperman, Norvell Wordsworth Page. He had just sold a grisly horror story, "Dance of the Skeletons," to Popular's *Dime Mystery Magazine*. A fast and fertile writer, Page must have been a Godsend to *Spider* editor Rogers Terrill. He knocked out a wild Spider exploit called *Wings of the Black Death*, and the true era of *The Spider* had begun.

Under Page, Richard Wentworth, AKA the *Spider*, Master of Men, grew into even more of a Shadow impersonator—wearing a black opera cape, matching slouch hat, and laughing manically as he blazed away with his twin Colt .45 automatics. This funereal regalia Wentworth augmented by a long-haired fright wig and celluloid vampire fangs, the better to terrorize the Underworld. It was an underworld that sorely needed terrorizing too, given that Wentworth battled costumed characters like the Tarantula, the Living Pharaoh, the Bat-Man and a human robot named Iron Man. In his Depression-era youth, Stan Lee loved the *Spider*.

The *Spider* was no ordinary crimefighter. He was a driven man, violent, emotionally brittle, branded a criminal by police, and forever hunted by the lawless element.

"There's a madness that gets in me when the *Spider* walks...." Wentworth once admitted. In an era when pulp heroes were square-jawed, steely-eyed emotionally suppressed supermen, Wentworth was a passionate avenger. This introspective passage paints a clear portrait of a haunted hero:

He looked down at his hand clenched hard about the newspaper, and for once in his vigorous life self-doubt arose to assail him. How many years was it now since first he had donned the valorous garments of the Spider? What sort of man had he become? But he knew without introspection. He was a man in whose hand a gun was more familiar than the hand-clasp of a friend, whose life was spent amid horror and death, whose eyes could never gaze upon a fellow man without probing behind the mask of humdrum existence and wondering: Shall I someday be forced to kill this man? If someone looked at him steadily or curiously, as had that guard upon the subway, he must immediately think that they had recognized him for what he was, that he was in peril of death or arrest through the agency of the person who looked. All this, merely that he might serve an ideal of justice.

Oh, there had been personal reasons behind his initial foray beyond the law—a dear friend was being framed out of life and honor and home. And there had been the example of his father, who had died when Wentworth wasscarcely in his teens, a great lawyer murdered by criminals because he had dared defy them to save an innocent man they had made their scape-goat.

OVER the following ten years, Page ground out a steady stream of over-the-top *Spider* sagas, sometimes spelled by other writers when creative fatigue and psychic exhaustion took their toll. A highly emotional writer, Page identified with Wentworth, often delivering his manuscripts dressed up in the robes of the *Spider!* Once, he stopped writing the *Spider* for several months amid rumors of a nervous breakdown.

By the time the 1940s rolled around, Page had put much of his inner conflicts about remaining with the series behind him and rededicated himself to his alter-ego's monthly exploits.

"There was a time when the burden of writing yet one more *Spider* seemed too much to undertake," Page told one fan. "But I never feel that way anymore. I know now that the *Spider* actually does help people; that there are those who appreciate his idealism even though it is expressed in violence."

But this period coincided with an upheaval in the pulp magazine market. Superman, Batman, and Captain Marvel had appeared on the scene, and were luring away *Spider* readers, just as the *Spider* had captured *Shadow* loyalists. Sales began slumping. Readers were writing letters, pleading with Grant Stockbridge to give the Spider superpowers lest he be eclipsed by these boldly-costumed upstarts.

The powers at Popular Publications held firm. Publishing comic books was briefly considered, then rejected by Steeger, who felt it was beneath him. A superhero version of the *Spider* was considered but discarded when Popular decided against comics.

MATTERS began going critical as the year 1943 approached. America had entered World War II. On the one hand, soldiers were reading magazines in great numbers, pumping up circulation. On the other, paper was becoming scarce. Washington began rationing pulp paper, forcing publishers to cut back severely. Even a magazine as solid as *The Spider* was at risk.

Instead of recognizing reality, Popular Publications began to wonder if the problem lay with the author. As he approached the ten-year anniversary of *The Spider,* Norvell Page was still writing the kind of white-hot pulp he had made famous in the 1930s. Times had changed and pulp styles were smoothing out. Fast action writing was on the wane. More realistic fiction was emphasized. The old hard-boiled style, which editors called the bang-bang pulp story, was considered out of date.

At this time, the editor on *The Spider* was Robert Turner, a writer in his own right. In his autobiography, he described the shift in editorial emphasis:

> *The trend was away from the fast-paced, hard-boiled, action-for-action's-sake type of thing and was leaning more and more toward better characterization, less pulpy writing, and more emotional impact, involving real people in crime rather than the stock private investigators, although those were still in demand if they had something special to distinguish them.*

Turner began revising Page's manuscripts to bring them in line with what were seen as World War II-era standards of fiction. The result was to homogenize Page's distinct style. *Spider* fans might or might not have been happy with the result.

We don't know the exact circumstances of Donald G. Cormack's recruitment into the league of Spider authors. The two most prolific former Stockbridges had moved on, Emile C. Tepperman to script the radio dramas *Gangbusters* and *Suspense,* and Wayne Rogers, to manage a chain of Florida movie houses. So fresh blood was needed.

A lifelong resident of Manhattan, and 1927 graduate of Columbia University, Cormack had been writing since the mid-thirties and was a semi-regular contributor to Popular titles such as *Dime Mystery Magazine* and *Strange Detective Mysteries.* For *Terror Tales* and *Horror Stories*, he penned the kind of Weird Menace stories Norvell Page spewed out in great numbers at the beginning of his *Spider* career. There, he employed the byline, Donald Graham. Every previous *Spider* author dabbled in Weird Menace fiction. Cormack fit the profile of a typical Grant Stockbridge. So they gave him a shot at the *Spider*.

CORMACK turned in *Slaughter, Inc.* on February 17, 1943. Maybe it was exactly what they wanted, perhaps it wasn't up to the level of Norvell Page. They paid for it, so they must have planned to print it. But other factors were also operating. The War Production Board had been cutting paper allotments to magazine publishers since 1942. In January of '43, a further 10% cut was announced to take effect on April 1.

All over pulpdom, magazines were being scrutinized for cancellation. *The Spider* was one of the titles on the chopping block. The March issue was on the stands when Cormack turned in his tale. Up to that point, *The Spider* had been a reliable monthly title. But three months passed before the next issue appeared, cover-dated June. Had *The Spider* been cancelled, only to receive a reprieve? No one knows. But for the rest of the year, Popular issued it bi-monthly.

According to the order of submission, *Slaughter, Inc.* should have appeared in the August issue. But a new Norvell Page story ran instead. Page kept grinding them out. Turner kept revising them. *Slaughter, Inc* was held back, perhaps against the day Norvell page might be drafted. All through 1942-43, writers were going into the service in droves.

THEN tragedy struck. Norvell Page's wife, Audrey, stepped on a rusty nail while gardening. Tetanus set in and she died in October. Page was understandably shattered.

Writing the *Spider* became impossible.

With his close friend, Shadow writer Theodore Tinsley, Page relocated to Washington D.C., to work for the Office of War Information. They lived two blocks apart. *The Spider* ceased publication with its December issue. Maybe it would have been killed anyway, but without Norvell Page, the soul of the *Spider*, there was no point in carrying on.

Donald G. Cormack's orphan *Spider* manuscript went into a drawer and stayed there for decades. The paper cuts of World War II knocked so many pulp markets out from under him that Cormack went on to other things. He had toiled on the staff of *Look* magazine. At the time of his untimely death in 1956, Cormack was an assistant editor of *Esquire*. He was only 45.

But that was not the end of the story of *Slaughter, Inc.* Decades later, a photocopy was smuggled out of the Popular offices and surreptitiously published by the short-lived Python Books as *Legend in Blue Steel*. Sporting an unpublished George Gross cover to an Operator #5 reprint cancelled by Freeway Press, it appeared in 1979 with all traces of its Spidery origins obliterated. Richard Wentworth was renamed Elsevier van Rijn, and his alter ego was the feared crimefighter known only as Blue Steel. The inspiration for the name, Blue Steel, came from a variant title of one of Steeger's old gangster pulps. Although the novel was credited to "Spider Page," few people who purchased the book back then were in on its secret history.

UNTIL now *Slaughter, Inc.* has never been printed in book form as it was written in 1943. Restored to its original state as a Richard Wentworth adventure, here it is—the last authentic *Spider* story. Moonstone Books is proud to publish it.

Will Murray
February 6, 2012

SLAUGHTER, INC.

I

Enter the Spider

THE deep-throated song of the Daimler limousine's powerful motor was a muted thunder in the narrowly, quiet side streets of the city's lower east side. Darkness pressed in on all sides. But, even if the dwellers of this slum section slept, danger and evil were awake—and it was toward the source of danger and evil that the Daimler now sped.

A young girl drove the car, alone in the front seat, her actions precise and confident. The other passenger of the car, a man, sat in the rear. He was keen-faced; and in his repose he gave one the impression of a sheathed sword, hinting of swift action and quick death on an instant's notice. A faint smile brushed his lips now as he peered into the onrushing darkness ahead, seeing there the promise of coming action.

"I might have known it!" the girl chided suddenly. "As soon as you called me, Dick, and told me to meet you with the car—I knew you were looking for trouble again!"

Richard Wentworth laughed easily—partly, perhaps, to hide his mounting tension. "We always fight the good and just battle, Nita. This time, I'm afraid, we enter it rather late. The forces of evil have had too much time in which to prepare and organize. Even so, you know you could no more stay out of it than I.”

Nita van Sloan's quick interest thrust aside her earlier fear for the man she loved. “The recent wave of seemingly unrelated and motiveless, murders—” she began.

“Exactly!” Wentworth corroborated. “They're not motiveless, they're not unrelated! I'm certain, now, that they're all part of a huge scheme—a plan so mad in its gigantic scope as to blind the orthodox mind of the law!”

“Over twenty murders in the past ten days, and the number increasing daily,” Nita recalled, speaking half to herself. “And you think you can prove your suspicions tonight, Dick?”

Richard Wentworth nodded grimly in the darkness of the car. “Tonight—now!” he said in a soft voice that was ominous in its quiet restraint.

“Just be careful, Dick—for the sake of those who love you,” was all she said. But it was a warning from her heart.

Nita van Sloan dreaded that one awful day when Richard Wentworth, as the *Spider*, might embark on a fight against the underworld that would never be marked closed. It seemed inevitable that such a time—and such a battle would ever come, in view of the fantastic odds that opposed the man she loved, and his allies— odds that he challenged with an eager, contemptuous pride.

Wentworth, the lone wolf of justice, struck wherever criminals preyed on innocent people. It was he whom the underworld feared most. Yet the police, who should have welcomed him to their ranks, tried to destroy him because he held that justice was not blind; that it was only the stupid administration of law that had made it seem so. His ways of dealing with the underworld were unorthodox and bold—and his was a higher, more terrible justice. The justice of the *Spider*!

Silence held in the car now, but Wentworth had not been idle. Swiftly, he had stripped of the dinner jacket he had worn to his club earlier that night. From a concealed compartment set in the rear of the front seat he had removed a dark yet flashily cut suit of the type favored by the underworld. This he put on, along with a loud-colored shirt and tie.

Another compartment revealed a self-illuminating mirror, tubes of grease paint, dyes, gum Arabic, and the other paraphernalia of disguise. Wentworth's fingers moved swiftly and expertly. Under his deft touches his strongly handsome young face began to change in contour and complexion. Ordinarily ruggedly healthy, his face was now drawn and white, with blue rings under the eyes. It was the face of a man who has lived much within prison walls and who ventures into the open only at night. A harmless drug had removed the challenging sparkle from his clear brown eyes; they were now blood-shot and dull.

When he finally nodded with satisfaction at his reflection, he was no longer Richard Wentworth, fashionable clubman and wealthy young-man-about-town. He was the cruel-faced, suspicious Blinky McQuade, a notorious identity Wentworth had built up in the underworld—and a character that had served him well.

As Blinky McQuade, Wentworth could venture into the lowest dives unchallenged. Gangsters, both big-shots and punks, acknowledged him as one of them and even offered him a certain grudging respect. He was known to work alone, and to do his own killing, when necessary. He was a touchy, surly character, so sensitive of his own anonymity that he was constantly on the arrogant defensive. It was best, the underworld whispered, to leave him completely alone. He wanted it that way.

Now, at Dick's direction, Nita drew the Daimler smoothly up to the curb. When she heard the rear door open and close, she lowered the bullet-proof window beside her and looked out. And, although she knew perfectly well who it was, she couldn't suppress a start of surprise when she saw Dick in his new identity. His uncanny ability to assume and actually live the character of another always affected her that way.

"My!" she whispered, with a forced little laugh. "How you've changed, Mr. Wentworth!" Then, more intensely, her voice breaking just a bit, "Oh, Dick, darling, please be..."

"...careful," he interrupted, ending the sentence for her. "I know, dear. And I promise. Meantime, I have to play this hand alone—and to have the car parked here might be a give-away. Run it back to the garage, Nita, and I'll meet you and Ram Singh at the apartment in an hour or two."

Swiftly, briefly, his lips brushed hers and then he had turned and was vanishing down the night-shrouded street. Behind him he heard the big Daimler purr softly into motion and he knew he was alone, headed for battle.

Excitement began to make Wentworth's pulses drum with long, slow, heavy throbs. He loved a fight. He was the Master of Men. He was the *Spider*.

THE EAST SIDE Bar hung out no neon sign to invite prospective customers inside. Situated below street level, only a faint glow of light seeped through its dirty, half-painted windows to illuminate the short flight of steps that led down to the entrance. One would have thought such an establishment would have failed quickly for lack of trade.

New customers, strangers, were exactly what the East Side Bar didn't want. A hang-out for the dregs of the underworld, those who came to the bar were old habitués and they came there either because it was a comparatively inconspicuous place in which to drink, or because they had a quiet conversation to hold, well away from listening ears. Even so, tense suspicion, taut danger, always seemed to quiver in the room.

Wentworth, as Blinky McQuade, stepped quickly through the

front door, halting abruptly as he let it swing closed behind him. Swiftly, his eyes flicked over the faces of those present, checking his society before he advanced any further—and his was a typical entrance. His reception was typical, too. As soon as he appeared at the end of the room, all conversation stopped and every eye jumped to identify the newcomer. In some eyes there was an immediate fear that slowly faded; in others there was but cautious suspicion; in all there was an alert tension.

For a second or two the rigid tableau held, then broke slowly as Blinky shuffled down to an open spot at the bar and eased himself against it. The murmur of conversation picked up again as the bartender came down and raised his eyes in interrogation, without speaking. For answer, Blinky slid a dime toward the beer taps and grunted.

For the next few minutes Blinky was apparently concerned with sipping his beer and in tracing designs on the wet bar with a forefinger, lost in thought. But actually excitement was rising inside him. His information had been correct! Tony Nucco was at the end of the bar, well apart from the others and at the extreme end of the room from the entrance, a whiskey bottle and glass standing in front of him.

Nucco was as tough as the underworld made them. Bull necked and with the chest of an ape, he iron-ruled his vicious gang with the authority of his huge fists, a knife or a gun. But tonight he didn't look so tough, even though he was apparently trying to steel his nerve with alcohol's false courage. It wasn't working. Through his dark-complexioned skin a livid fear was showing. His big hands trembled slightly as he tossed down drink after drink. Behind his small black eyes a brooding terror could be seen.

Wentworth knew he had reached the beginning of the trail—a trail that promised fantastic twists before he reached its hell-spawned conclusion. Why, otherwise, should Nucco—cruel bully among ruthless killers—visibly shake with terror? There could be but one reason! Tony Nucco had come up against someone or something a hundred times more vicious than he! And at the thought of that fantastic menace Blinky McQuade's lips grew grimly taut.

So far, his information had been correct. Nucco, mad-dog mob leader, was behaving like a child with a nightmare. The rest, then, might be true as well. Although it had been withheld from the public, Wentworth had learned from another source that the police had reason to suspect Nucco of complicity in one of the recent killings in the present murder-wave. The police were looking for him.

Obviously, though, Nucco wasn't afraid of the police. He was contemptuous of them. Once picked up, he'd never talk. And, since his terror must spring from the very menace that Wentworth had sworn to exterminate, he had to make Nucco talk before it was too late!

For perhaps fifteen minutes Blinky McQuade stood quietly at the bar, his presence now accepted and forgotten. Then, casually, he picked up his glass of beer and drifted down the bar toward the bulking figure of the gang leader.

Tony Nucco's small eyes darted toward him, bright and hard, as he sidled up. The muscles of his jaw tightened.

"Greetings, Tony," Blinky's flat, hard voice said. "You alone tonight? Thought you wouldn't mind..."

"I do," Nucco announced coldly. "Beat it, Blinky. Fade. Tonight I want alone. Get it?"

Instant anger flared in Blinky eyes. He wasn't the sort who could be talked to that way. Springing from Tony's fear or not, Blinky McQuade wouldn't take it.

"I don't like that brush-off, Nucco," he said; icy threat chilling his words. "I don't like it! Get it?"

"No?" Nucco's hand nudged slightly toward his underarm holster, then froze. The gaze of the two men tangled, locked, and

Wentworth's muscles steeled for impending action. Finally, Nucco's eyes jumped back to the entrance door, ever apprehensive.

"Scram, Blinky," he breathed heavily. "I'm warning you now, ape! Scram!"

It was then Wentworth noticed the dead, tight silence in the room. He knew everyone there was aware of the clash between the two men and he knew that Nucco's pride wouldn't let him back down, any more than the pride of McQuade would allow. He couldn't retreat—he couldn't shoot it out with Nucco, who had to live—and he had to make the vicious gangster talk freely!

2

DEATH'S DEPUTY

WENTWORTH let the tension seep from his action-ready muscles. He laughed shortly, without humor. "Okay, sucker," he breathed in a whisper. "If you want it that way. If you want to take what's coming instead of listening to a compromise, even when the offer comes straight from—him! I got nothing to..."

"Wait!" Nucco interrupted. "What's this all about? Who's offering me the compromise?"

"You know as much about him as I do," Blinky said meaningfully. "And as little. Why bother about that now? You either want to hear or you don't. I'm only the messenger, but it's your funeral! Well, think it over, pal—while you still can."

When the burly gang-leader said "wait" a second time, Wentworth felt a new excitement. His chance shot had found the mark. It was almost pitiful to see Nucco's reaction. Sweat beaded his face and his tongue licked repeatedly at his livid, dry lips. Also, the attention of the others in the room had now drifted away from the two men and an immediate showdown had been averted.

"Let's hear your piece," Tony Nucco demanded at last. "What am I offered besides a free ride in the meat wagon?"

"Not here, you dope!" Blinky snapped—and at the same time he reached in front of Nucco to take one of the cigarettes from the pack lying beside the whiskey bottle. "I've got a little room just around the corner where we can..."

Nucco's harsh laugh interrupted him. The gangster picked up his shot glass, snapped back his head, and downed the drink in a gulp. Then he looked back at Blinky, his eyes were blazing with suspicion and anger. He ripped out a few sulfurous oaths.

"The old double-cross, is that it, you rat! And of all the dumb tries I ever heard of! You want me to walk right into a little tommy-gun party so we can compromise. Why, you dirty..."

A queer expression twisted his face then and a new terror came into his eyes. The terror of seeing approaching death. His right arm jumped toward his gun, but for a man notoriously quick on the draw his movement was comparatively slow. Wentworth's cable-tendoned fingers had plenty of time to flash forward and seize the wrist, hold it from sight beneath the bar.

Tony Nucco's bulging eyes twisted up from his imprisoned wrist to rest beseechingly on Blinky's. Twice his knotted throat convulsed in an effort to speak, but no words came. Slowly, his heavy body tilted toward the bar. Still upright, eyes still open, he remained there motionless, seemingly paralyzed.

For the briefest part of a second Blinky McQuade's eyes were those of Richard Wentworth, flashing in triumph. The capsule he had palmed and dropped into Nucco's drink as he reached for that cigarette had worked just barely in time. The powerful hypnotic it contained — hyocyamus — would leave a man all but paralyzed and unable to speak. It was far more effective than the usual chloral hydrate, which left its victim an unconscious hulk.

"Come on, Tony," Blinky urged loudly. "Let's get out of here. You need some sleep; you can't drink like that forever. Hell, guy, no girl is worth it! Let's go."

A few half-curious glances raised at McQuade's remarks, but nothing was said as he assisted the tottering, bug-eyed gangster toward the door. If any of them had a suspicion of what was happening to the gangster, none arose to interfere. After all, none of Tony's gang was here and these kind of men didn't meddle in other business, even though they may have long since suspected Tony Nucco was on the dead-man's spot.

Outside, Richard Wentworth ignored the cab that flipped its door open invitingly just in front of the exit. Even had he needed transportation he would have been wary of such a possible trap as that. He was well aware that others beside the police were searching for Nucco and he knew they'd stop at nothing to succeed in seizing him. But when he'd told the other man at the bar that he had a room just around the corner, he'd been telling the truth. It was a sanctuary he'd used in the past when on such excursions as this—and it was stocked with the needs for any emergency.

Once around the nearest corner, Blinky doubled back sharply with the reeling Nucco and peered cautiously around the corner. It may have been a trick of the shadows but he thought he caught a flicker of movement paralleling the course he had just taken down the street. Had Tony Nucco left some of his own men outside for protection? But that wasn't possible. If Nucco had been terrified of something, his men would be caught doubly in the grip of terror. They'd be useless for protection. So there was only one other possible explanation.

Wentworth was being trailed by the henchmen of that very power which had all but driven Tony Nucco out of his mind!

There would be no turning back now, though because Richard Wentworth never turned back! Lifting the burly figure of Nucco with effortless ease, draping him over his shoulders, he sped down the side street for twenty yards and then seemingly vanished from sight!

This was his usual entrance to the hideout, though the back alley route. Because of that method, however, working almost the full length of the block through the tortuous passageways and fence-blocked back yards of the adjoining tenement houses, he was certain he had never been trailed.

Moments later a sharp-eared listener might have heard the faintest whisper of footsteps on stairs followed by the soft closing and bolting of a door somewhere in that block of ancient, rabbit-warren hovels.

Dick Wentworth's first play in this new game had been successful, a game in which the stakes were the triumph of justice and right—or of evil and death!

Nucco, all but unconscious now, lay sprawled on a cot in the room. Seemingly with sightless eyes he gazed straight upward at the ceiling. Wentworth, meantime, had stepped quickly to a small medicine cabinet hanging over the small wash-basin at one side of the room. He saturated a towel with a prepared chemical solution he kept there, then briskly scrubbed his face. Rapidly, the drawn, cruel features of Blinky McQuade disappeared and the handsome face of Richard Wentworth came to view.

Seconds later, Richard Wentworth was again busily altering his features with swift, deft touches. Knowing that every moment now counted, he shrugged quickly out of the suitcoat he had been wearing, strode to a hidden compartment in the rear of the closet and removed a tight bundle of clothes.

In almost the time it takes to tell, the transformation was complete. In the center of the room stood a man robed in black. His face was shadowed by a broad-brimmed hat, but his eyes glittered. They were cold and full of menace. A jet-black cape belled from his shoulders and death itself could be no more terrible than his lined and bloodless face. The face of the *Spider*!

Wentworth had known that Tony Nucco would not break down

easily. If the police had not been able to do it in the past, no ordinary threat would be great enough to make him talk now. There was only one fearful threat great enough to shake the mankind of anyone in the city, criminal or not. The threat of the *Spider*!

Returning to the medicine cabinet, the *Spider* withdrew a hypodermic needle and a small vial, from which he filled the needle. It was an antidote for the hyocyamus he had introduced into Tony Nucco's drink; it would assure his recovery in a matter of moments. Administering the drug in the fleshy part of the thug's upper arm, he stepped back to the center of the room and stood there waiting, arms folded.

Suddenly, Nucco began to blink rapidly and shake his head, as though chasing the last mists of semi-consciousness from his brain. He stretched his arms and legs once, apparently not remembering what had happened in the bar, and began slowly to haul himself upright, grunting sleepily. Abruptly, though, his side-vision caught a glimpse of the second figure in the room and his eyes swiveled toward it in quick fear—and then those eyes strained open to their widest, bulging, and he snapped bolt upright on the bed. Terror made his jaw gape foolishly; terror clutched at his throat; only terror prevented a scream from breaking from his throat. When sound did come from him it was a hoarse croak:

"The *Spider*!"

The *Spider* laughed, whisperingly. "Your host, Nucco. And, unless our conference is entirely satisfactory to me—your executioner as well!" He gestured negligently with the gun he held loosely at his side. "Shall we proceed, Nucco?"

A fit of insanity seemed to seize the gang leader then. With a wild leap he hurled himself from the bed, as though to send his body crashing through the window. But the *Spider* moved with incredible speed. With his left hand he seized the other's wrist, twisted, held him like that, immovably, kneeling at his feet.

"The *Spider*!" Nucco repeated, babbling. "Then they were right! That's what was whispered around! The *Spider's* behind the whole thing! Dwyer told me..." But sudden sanity seemed to warn him and he cut off his words.

Nucco tried to look away from the eyes that blazed down into his, but he couldn't. They held his sight as a magnet holds a needle. The face above seemed to shimmer before him: that lipless gash of a mouth that scarcely opened when the *Spider* spoke; that predatory beak of a nose.

"What did Dwyer tell you?" the command came now. "Speak!"

Cold, merciless fury was in the *Spider's* voice. This was an old trick of the underworld—to blame any infamous series of crimes on the *Spider*, to brand his name with the origin of the very evil he risked his life to combat.

"What did Dwyer..." he began to repeat and then it happened!

The sudden crash of gunfire filled the room, Nucco's shriek mingling with the harsh reverberations, and in the same instant the *Spider's* hair-trigger reaction had carried him over to the light switch with a bound. The room plunged into darkness.

A second chattering series of shots followed the first volley, but by that time the *Spider* had all but reached the window. The shards of splintered glass that filled the room crunched and broke under his feet. Then, with unbelievable abruptness, the *Spider* was no longer in the room. A single leap had carried him through the empty window frame and out onto the fire escape, where he landed with feline grace, gun ready for action.

The fire escape was empty. A glance told the *Spider* that no one had scurried down the ladder and into the alley below. An open window across the way could have been the source of the shots—or the killers could have scurried up the two remaining flights and onto the roof above. A quick search showed the roof to be empty too— and further chase would be pointless. These men were only cheap killers; it was the ones that did the hiring that the *Spider* wanted to get his hands on.

Returning to the shambles of the room, the *Spider* verified what he had been certain he would find; Tony Nucco dead, his paunchy body riddled with bullets. But he found something else, too— something he hadn't expected, and something that told him he was dealing with a far cleverer brand of criminal than he had at first expected. It showed a meticulous care for detail.

Burned into the center of Nucco's forehead was a crude imitation of the dread *Spider* symbol, its harsh red outline supposedly showing that violent justice has been meted out. But it was not a criminal brand, one to cover brutal murder! At sight of it, the *Spider's* fists clenched at his sides and his mouth grew harsh and grim.

The brand itself could be removed, he knew. It was the daring of the criminal maneuver that infuriated him. Further, the two cheap killers had undoubtedly been well rehearsed. One of them had blazed through the window with a tommygun, exterminating Nucco. Then, the room plunging into darkness as they'd expected, the second had slipped daringly into the room. The second blast of gunfire had been simply intended to lure the *Spider* into the open while the inside man counterfeited the brand on the corpse. Before the return of the *Spider* he had undoubtedly fled from the building by way of the door and inner stairway. It had been neat.

The *Spider* abruptly straightened at that point in his thoughts, every sense tingling alertly, danger quickening his pulse. That noise in the street outside, so quickly stilled! It had been the beginning wail of a police siren, frantically choked off! Was he at that moment in the center of a huge, closing trap?

Darkness dropped over the room as he thumbed out the light. A quick stride carried him to the window, where he peered cautiously out. The alley below whispered back echoes of muffled footfalls as a cordon of police filed silently to posts surrounding the building!

Others should be on the stairs by now, creeping up as they covered the house floor by floor—and the *Spider's* only last hope of escape, a faint and doubtful one, would be by way of the roof!

Not only was the corpse falsely branded with the seal of the *Spider*, but the police had been advised of his presence — and the *Spider* himself was trapped within a swiftly closing cordon of grimly determined men, each one swearing that this time the arch criminal would not again escape them!

3

TRAPPED AT LAST!

THERE was now no time to remove the false brand from Nucco's forehead; there was now time for nothing but escape—and probably not even enough for that!

Swift strides carried the *Spider* out into the hallway. One glance down into the stairwell showed him a pair of hands slowly advancing upward along the banister, the climbers themselves hidden from view. Below the advancing police, other blue-coated figures could be seen on the landings below. That way of escape was impossible, especially since the *Spider*, unlike his adversaries of the city force, refused to use his guns against them. The only way left was upward.

Pacing noiselessly, the *Spider* sped to the next flight of stair and disappeared upward, moving with incredible speed. One floor, then the top floor of that miserable dwelling felt his flying feet. The skylight to the roof—which way?

It was his urgent pace and the uncertain light of flickering gas jets that caused the accident, an accident of which he wasn't at first aware. He felt the gentle jar against his leg, but he didn't give it a second thought in passing. It was the sound of the little girl's heartbroken sobs that made him skid to a halt. Momentarily pausing, it took him a second even then to make out the ragged little form that was huddled against the wall. And, tenderness flooding him, he turned and walked back deliberately toward the crying youngster and toward the footfalls that now pounded openly and noisily upward!

He knelt beside her and lifted her to her feet, his hands under her frail little arms. "I'm sorry, Princess!" he said tenderly. "I didn't mean to knock you down. It was so dark. I didn't see."

"That's—that is all right," the girl told him between her sobs. "I'm—I'm all right. It's Mummy. You didn't hurt me. It's Mummy. Oh, I'm so afraid!"

Downstairs a thunderous crashing noise told of a locked door being smashed from its hinges. Behind that door lay the body of Nucco—bearing the false seal of the *Spider*!

"What about your Mummy?" the *Spider* urged. "Why does she make you afraid? And why are you crying?"

"She doesn't answer the door when I knock," the child told him, somewhat calmer now that an adult shared her problem. "She's home, though. I know that. And—and there's that funny smell of the stove coming through the door! I don't know what..."

"Then let's go quickly and tell Mummy about it," the *Spider* broke in—but forced his voice to remain calm so as not to frighten the little girl. "Fast, now! The stove needs fixing."

Gas! Seeping from the door in a tenement like this, it could mean but one thing! The child led him rapidly to a doorway at the extreme end of the gloomy corridor. Beside it ran a ladder leading to the skylight and escape just above. The *Spider* didn't look at it twice.

The door was locked, all right. Gripping the knob firmly, the *Spider* began to twist. The smooth muscles of his arm ridged, knotted; color mounted in his face and the veins in his temple stood out sharply. Then there was a cracking snap of metal and wood as the lock disintegrated under the terrific pressure—and the door swung limply inward.

32

Warning the girl to stay in the outer room, the *Spider* went quickly through to the kitchen. His first move was to throw open the window there, calling to the girl to open the one in the wretched living room, and then he was picking up the limply unconscious form that slumped over the gas stove.

The gas jets turned off, there was only one other possible move for the *Spider* to make. Artificial respiration. It was the white-faced, young-looking woman's only hope now. As he placed her prone upon the floor, beginning the intermittent pressure to induce forced breathing, he saw the pitiful note she had scrawled for the police. It was the usual thing. No money...a child to take care of...the hope that her death would place the little girl in the hands of someone better able to care for her....

The police were on the upper floor now, going from apartment to apartment in their systematic search. Others, too, had gained the roof; their crunching footsteps overhead were plainly audible. The police above, below, in the street outside, overhead! There could be no possible escape for the *Spider* now. Even his silken web couldn't accomplish the miracle of carrying him out of a solid square block of alert police—who knew he was within reach!

The *Spider* saw no way. He was trapped at last.

The artificial respiration he administered began to show results at last. The air of the room now clear of the fatal monoxide fumes, color began to show in the young woman's face again. But she was still in serious condition; she couldn't yet breathe by herself. And the police were already searching the apartment next door! They'd be in this very one within minutes!

"Princess!" the *Spider* called suddenly. "Come here a minute, will you?" Then, when she'd entered the kitchen, looking wide-eyed and uncomprehending at her mother, the *Spider* explained in a reassuring voice, "Mummy's all right. She's fine. But she's fallen into a very deep sleep and we've got to awaken her, but I need help to do that. So will you play a little game with me?"

The little girl, gaining strength and confidence from the *Spider's* easy tone, nodded brightly. "You bet!"

''Listen carefully, then. I want you to go out in the hall and get one of those men in uniform to one side. Just one, mind you! We don't want any more in here. And you tell him just what you told me—exactly the same. Only don't mention that I'm here! If you do, he might not think you need help badly enough. Just tell him your Mummy is asleep and the smell of the stove is all over the house. Quick, now!"

After she had run to play her part of the game, the *Spider* ceased his artificial respiration— and sighed with relief when he saw the labored, but natural, rise and fall of her chest as the paralyzing effects of the monoxide was thrown off. But he himself was no better off! He might just as well be trapped in a center room of the headquarters building!

Nor did the *Spider* dare reassume the identity of Richard Wentworth; such a move would be fatal. Captured as Wentworth— and surrounded by evidence of the *Spider*—the two names would be positively linked, something no policeman, high or low, had ever been able to do. Suspicion? Yes. There was plenty of that—but no proof!

Stanley Kirkpatrick, Police Commissioner of New York and Dick Wentworth's warm friend, would have given his eye-teeth— and maybe a few front ones too—to have the proof of what he suspected so strongly: that Richard Wentworth and the *Spider* were one and the same. Nor would he let friendship stand in the way of duty once that fact was established. Tall, soldierly, rigidly honest, the Commissioner was an implacable instrument of the law as it is written in the law books.

Footsteps in the outer room caused the *Spider* to move quickly against the wall and directly beside the swinging door leading into the kitchen. The cop entered alone, his eyes going immediately to the form of the now-reviving woman sprawled face-down on the floor. Then he turned, fast, perhaps warned by some whisper of sound behind him, prompted of danger by his taut nerves.

He was too late. With a murmured, "Sorry, old man," the *Spider's* darting fingers caught him at the base of the skull, pressed there with gentle science and the policeman's eyelids fluttered closed as swift unconsciousness swept over him.

After that the *Spider's* movements were urgently swift. He cast off the black robes and cape of the *Spider*, then stooped over the unconscious man and stripped him of his uniform, putting its generous size on right over his own suit. The clumping sound of heels in the hallway outside told him the police had finished searching the apartment next door. But there was one last act he had to perform.

A small kit in his pocket gave him the material to remove the *Spider* make-up he still wore, and the officer's cap sufficiently concealed his hair and eyes to get him past cursory inspection in the dim hallway outside. But what would happen when the unconscious cop was found? He wouldn't be half way out of the building by that time, much less clear of the cordoned blocks

A faint smile brushed across Wentworth's features as the solution came to him. The kit was in his hand again and within a few seconds the limp form of the policeman was swathed in the *Spider's* robes, his face hastily dabbed with make-up to give it a fair resemblance to that of the *Spider*!

When he entered the dingy living room, the child came to her feet quickly. "You're not leaving?" she asked. "Aren't you going to help that nice man wake my Mummy up? He said he needed..."

Dick Wentworth realized she mistook him for the policeman, which was logical. "She's awake now, kiddie," he told her. "You can go in and see her if you want. But first I want you to do something for me." His hand was in his pocket and pulling out his wallet. He handed her a wad of bills. "Give this present to her after the other men leave, will you?"

The child's eyes were large with disbelief as she took the money he offered; she knew what it was, even at her age. But she had probably learned through first knowing what the tragic lack of it can mean... hunger and want.

A group of police were already at the door when Wentworth opened it. His appearance surprised them since the house was being searched apartment by apartment, a squad to each floor.

"What the devil are you doing here?" the sergeant in charge demanded. "Whose squad are you detailed to?"

Wentworth thought fast. "I'm a new man, sir; the beat patrolman in this section. One of the neighbor's kids came to me and reported that her mother had fainted when an intruder entered their home. I came to investigate, and she was telling the truth. The intruder was still there, too. He got tough so I slugged him out and thought I'd turn him over to you." Then, before the sergeant exploded with anger, Wentworth added innocently: "He's a mighty queer looking duck, Sergeant, wearing black robes, a cape and a big floppy black hat. He's in the kitchen now. I wish you'd..."

The rush of the police into the apartment slammed Wentworth against the wall in their eagerness. But Wentworth didn't follow. A broad smile on his lips, he walked down the empty hallway and started down the stairs. Excited shouts—mixed with understandable jubilation— reached his ears as he gained the next floor below. The *Spider* had been captured at last! Or so they thought.

A police captain stood on the outer front steps and Wentworth saluted smartly as he passed. The officer watched his trim figure and athletic, soldierly stride as Wentworth disappeared down the street. A glint of approval shone in his eye.

"Who's that?" he asked a lieutenant. "A new man?"

"Must be, sir," the lieutenant told him. "Never saw him before.

But he's a likely looking lad. Good material, that."

"Glad he joined the force," the captain replied—and then the news reached them from upstairs. The *Spider* had been caught! They forgot then about the new addition to the New York Police.

But they'd remember him shortly, though with different sentiments about his joining the force, however briefly.

Ten minutes later Richard Wentworth was in the telephone booth of an uptown cafe. The sophisticated music from the dance floor drifted pleasantly into the lobby, its muted strains plainly audible to anyone listening on the other end of the mire.

"Hello, Kirk," Wentworth drawled easily. "Thought I could catch you at your office at this moment. How are things going?"

"What made you think I'd be at my office, Dick?" The sharp suspicion in Commissioner Kirkpatrick's tones was evident.

"Oh, a rumor I heard, old man. Something about the *Spider* being caught in a police trap. Can't keep that sort of thing a secret, you know. Any truth in it?"

"You ought to know, Dick!" Kirkpatrick snapped.

Wentworth laughed quietly. "Still keeping up that old joke, eh, Kirk? Why don't you forget it!"

The Commissioner left the phone hurriedly then, asking Dick to hold on, a sure sign an important official report had come through on his private wire. Dick Wentworth leisurely tapped a cigarette on a silver case as he waited, a faint smile on his lips. He knew what that report could be. The *Spider* had been captured! Some excited sergeant would be apt to phone it in before the hoax had been discovered.

"Dick, you there?" Kirkpatrick voice came back after moments. "Look, boy, call me back later. I've just received an important flash; got to rush along." His voice sounded suddenly weary and he hung up without further ceremony.

Stanley Kirkpatrick would investigate that flash, of course. But in his heart, deep, he'd know it was a futile chase; hadn't he just been speaking to Dick Wentworth on another wire?

But Commissioner Kirkpatrick was a patient man. He could wait. And a day would come....

By the time Wentworth had reached the street his face was grim again. In spite of his escape, in spite of his temporary triumph over Kirkpatrick, he had progressed very little this night. There was still the threat of mass murders hanging over the city—and he had done little yet to smash it. All he knew was a single name: Dwyer. That indicated his next move.

His lips were tightly set as he signaled a cab and swung lithely into the back seat. There was work to be done, a coming battle to be won—and damn the odds!

4

INTO BATTLE

THERE was but one Dwyer in the city who could be the person
the doomed Nucco had referred to: William "Big Bill" Dwyer.
His was a strange past—and an equally strange present. A
product of the city's slums, he hadn't profited by that background
after his rise to political power, as have so many others with a like
origin. His character was partly that of the cheap politician, partly
that of a borderline gangster, and he frequently acted as "middleman"
in fostering criminal deals mutually profitable to both such groups.

During the cab ride downtown Wentworth bought a newspaper
from a passing newsboy, glanced swiftly at the headlines as they
lurched into motion again. And this early morning edition only
confirmed the fears he'd expressed to Nita hours before.

Three more wanton murders were reported— and, as in the
score already committed, the same puzzling fact appeared, linking
them all as the work of a single organization! In no case was the
victim in any way connected with the underworld— nor was there
any apparent profit to the underworld in the deaths!

It almost looked as though some crime empire had gone
completely mad, killing for the sheer joy of it. And it was the work
of professional killers in each instance; that much was obvious in

the handicraft of the crimes.

Nine had been killed in Manhattan; three in the Bronx; five in Brooklyn; two on Long Island— on and on the list read. Some of the victims had money, true—but others were comparatively poor. But none of them was in any way connected with another—nor in any way with the underworld itself.

Here was a highly dangerous situation. A few more days of such reports and stark panic would strike the heart of the city, the greatest metropolis of the world. What a blow to the national war effort were such a thing to happen! Yet Richard Wentworth was positive sabotage was not the purpose of the kill-mad criminals. They had but one motive: profit of some sort. But what kind of profit could be found behind these crimes?

One other fact struck Wentworth as he tossed the newspaper aside. In addition to the murder of innocent citizens, two other out-and-out gang slayings had been reported. The fact that made these worthy of note was simple: in each instance the criminals involved were being sought by the District Attorneys office for questioning in the present crime wave. They had been reported on or near the scene of one of the recent murders. Just as Tony Nucco had been sought. And found—dead!

There was no report yet that the *Spider* was the man thought by the police to be behind the mass assassinations. That angle was probably being withheld for a time, which only made the implications for Richard Wentworth's future more ominous still.

Then Wentworth was alighting from the cab in the downtown slum. Here Dwyer had been born—and here, through some quirk of vanity, he continued to live. His strange ego had even insisted on selecting the same moldering ruin which had been the tenement in which he had been born.

Wentworth's step was thoughtful as he entered the building, climbed the creaking, uncarpeted stairs to the narrow, odorous hallway above. Unshaded gas jets lighted the way at irregular intervals and Wentworth walked unhesitatingly to a door at the far end of the corridor. It was his business to know the whereabouts of certain key figures in crime, and to know something of their background, as well.

Unlike the other scarred, unpainted doors that lined the hall, Dwyer enjoyed the luxury of a push-bell. In answer to the pressure of his finger, soft chimes sounded within—and after a brief space of time a butler in full livery opened the door! The frozen-faced manservant extended a silver tray respectfully toward Wentworth, and he, equally expressionless, dropped a card on it and turned toward an easy chair in the foyer hall as Dwyer's man disappeared into the inner room.

Dwyer had lavished money on his egotistical palace-in-a-slum; that much was obvious, so obvious, in fact, that Richard Wentworth had to smile at the blatant show of poor breeding.

"I wonder why he bothered removing the price tags in the first place?" he murmured, removing his gloves slowly.

The walls, once a cracked-plaster disgrace, were now paneled from floor to ceiling in solid mahogany; rich, deep carpets covered the floor, each color clashing with the next; the furniture, all expensive, was a mixture of style periods all the way from Sheraton and Queen Anne to the most fantastic modern. It was an interior decorator's nightmare. "Mr. Dwyer is in, Mr. Wentworth. This way, please."

Wentworth walked through into the living room and saw Dwyer standing at the far end, the mere sight of him arousing revulsion. His flabby face, moist and white as a fish's belly, was cut by a lipless gash of a mouth and two shoe-button eyes. Now he had struck an obviously assumed pose, a cigar jutting upward from one corner of his mouth, head thrust forward, hands clasped behind his back. He probably thought he was copying the forceful stance of England's Prime Minister Churchill.

"Yes?" he demanded briefly.

Richard Wentworth's gaze held his for a moment, and then Dwyer's eyes wavered and fell. He abandoned his pose, one chubby hand fumbling the cigar from his mouth as an obviously false laugh sounded mechanically in his throat.

"Well," he said with assumed joviality. "Well, Mr. Wentworth! And what makes you honor my humble quarters this evening?"

Richard Wentworth lowered himself slowly into an easy chair, a superior, mocking smile on his lips. Twice he flicked his gloves against the knife-like crease ridging his crossed knee.

"Trouble, Dwyer," he replied quietly. "Trouble—and the promise of much more to come. I thought either you would try to help me— or share some of it with me!"

Dwyer turned his laugh on again, but his beady eyes were sharp and alive behind their folds of fat. He was far from being a stupid man; he hadn't risen to his present position by making mistakes. And he could be very dangerous; none but a ruthless man mixes in the society of gangsters—and teaches them to obey him.

"Ah," he said noncommittally. "Trouble. By that, I suppose you refer to this present regrettable crime wave in the city. Why, only an hour ago I was listening to that new would-be reformer, Silas Breen, spouting over the radio. You know, the guy who turned up lately and began hiring halls all around the city to tell people the price of sin, urging them to rehabilitate their criminal fellows through concrete help and then passing the hat for a bit of concrete help for himself?"

"Well, he had an interesting point, Wentworth. A very interesting point! He said that maybe this new crime wave, whether a visitation of God or not, might be a very good thing! Know his reason? He pointed out that every city reform movement sprang from just such a condition as exists now! And he's right! An aroused common people, a fighting-mad John-Q-Citizen, can be a terribly tough guy when he wants to be. His millions can stamp out any crime empire ever dreamed of, Wentworth!"

Richard Wentworth smiled thinly. "And you're telling me that, I suppose, to convince me you couldn't have a hand in what's going on—because it would eventually interfere with your graft and corrupt political machines?"

Big Bill Dwyer didn't bat an eye. "Exactly!" he agreed. "You understood my point even before I made it!"

"Perhaps," Wentworth murmured, "I also understood your point a bit further than you intended. Because you could very easily be involved in the present chaos—if you stood to gain thereby more than you could possibly gain through your rotten graft!"

Dwyer was visibly shaken; the thrust had gotten in under his guard. Following his advantage, Wentworth pressed on. "Dwyer , what do you know about Tony Nucco? What was he so terrified of and why was he executed? Who's the man who's bossing you?"

Dwyer's face was frozen now; it was an experienced poker face he'd used before grand juries and investigating committees. "I know nothing about Nucco!" he snapped. Your other questions don't even make sense!"

"You know nothing about Nucco," Wentworth repeated, "except that he hated your guts—and that he owed you ten thousand dollars!"

Sweat glistened on Dwyer's face now; his back was to the wall. He could feel the force of Wentworth's personality, the strength of his magnificent will, slowly overcoming him. And he was desperate in the emergency. How could Richard Wentworth—graceful living, harmless and wealthy young clubman that he was—know these most secret facts about other's lives?

"Would I want him killed if he owed me that much money?" was all he could think of in reply.

"Dwyer, I haven't any more time to waste on you!" Wentworth

came to his feet now, his eyes hard. "I'm giving you one last chance. Who's your boss? If you don't tell me, I'll find out anyway— and when I return you'll regret the day you were born!"

Perspiration actually ran down Dwyer's face. One hand, deep in the pocket of his dressing gown, obviously gripped an automatic. But he said nothing. The dreadful look in his eyes was a reflection of Nucco's terror earlier that night. He stood motionless.

Richard Wentworth walked to the front door, opened it half way and then turned back to Dwyer again, leaning negligently against the jamb as he did so.

"Last chance, Dwyer," he said. "That boss of yours would turn you in just as fast as he turned

Nucco in tonight. Why don't you get smart and cross him up first?"

When Dwyer didn't answer, Wentworth walked out, closing the door quietly behind him. But he didn't walk down the hall. His real strategy had been to terrify Dwyer to a point where he'd immediately contact the man above him—and lead Wentworth as he did so. As an added precaution, Wentworth, while leaning so nonchalantly against the door jamb, had filled the latch behind him with a plastic substance that would prevent it from locking. The slightest pressure would open it now.

Wentworth didn't have long to wait. Almost immediately he heard the whirring of a phone dial—and partial disappointment came then. Dwyer's dial was especially constructed so that not even a person adept at the art, such as Wentworth, could not discover the number dialed by noting the varying number of clicks on dial-return. But the conversation itself might reveal everything. Wentworth nudged the door open a few inches as the conversation began.

"Boss? Dwyer. Wentworth was just here threatening. He has plenty of suspicions and he's apt to get right on the beam any hour now! What are we going to do?" A pause followed. "What! But that's impossible! You don't know the guy! You couldn't get him to join up with you for a..." Another pause—and then a jubilant laugh. "I get it! Oh, that is sweet! Nita van Sloan—and it's already arranged, eh? Wonderful!"

Red fury blazed up in Richard Wentworth's brain in that instant, leaving him momentarily frozen with fear for her. Nita! Some trap was being prepared for her—was already in process of execution! His own Nita!

By the heavens, now Dwyer would talk—or die!

It was then Wentworth heard the step behind him, whirled to see the butler crouched for a charge, knife in hand. He had turned just in time to avoid receiving the thrust in the back—but not in time to go for his own weapon. As the butler's brawny body hurtled straight at him in a practiced dive, Richard Wentworth suddenly fell to his knees as his arms shot upward under the flying figure, catching it chin and stomach. But, instead of retarding the man's flight, he expedited it by twisting and hurling as the body flew over his head. The crash of body against wall was thunderous in the narrow hall, and as it flopped

back limply to the floor the head was twisted at a queer angle.

But Wentworth didn't stop now. He raced to the apartment, straight-arming the door open to crash back against the wall, and charged into the living room. It was empty. The room beyond was empty...the bedrooms...the kitchen.... Richard Wentworth knew bitter, painful defeat then. Big Bill Dwyer had evidently had two apartments made into one, walls being knocked out to enlarge rooms. And in one of the bedrooms, behind a wall drape, he discovered the hidden door of the second apartment, leading into a second hallway. Warned by the sounds of the fight outside, he had evidently run for the emergency exit, escaped.

Was there still time to warn Nita of the threatening trap—a trap whose devilishness Wentworth could only guess at? The thought and the action were almost simultaneous. He raced to the foyer hall, swept up the phone and dialed the number of his apartment with a jabbing forefinger. Nita had said she'd wait for him there—would she have left for any reason? The interminable ringing of the unanswered phone was a death knell in Wentworth's ear—a death knell for those who plotted to harm the girl he loved!

But suddenly there was an answer. "Who rings?" a booming voice came over the wire. "Ram Singh speaks here."

Relief flooded through Wentworth, leaving him limp. "Ram Singh! Good old Ram Singh!" he greeted his faithful giant Sikh servant exuberantly. No harm could come to Nita while Ram Singh remained alive. "Let me speak with the missie sahib."

"Your joy is good to hear," the full-throated reply came. "But one fears it will not last. The missie sahib is not here."

"Not there, Ram Singh! When did she leave? Where did she go?"

"Those answers I do not know, sahib. I was performing an errand. I just returned as the phone was summoning. The missie sahib is not here, of that one I am sure."

"Ram Singh, wait there for me!" Wentworth ordered. "There is much trouble and the missie sahib is in danger!"

The Sikh's booming roar of anger still echoed in Wentworth's ear as he raced from the apartment and charged down to the street.

5

TRAP

AS ALWAYS, when Dick Wentworth had embarked on one of his dangerous solitary excursions into the underworld, Nita van Sloan was nervous, jittery. She longed to be with him, just to know from moment to moment that he was all right, but so often that was impossible. Such as tonight.

After garaging the car she returned to Dick's apartment, found no one answered her ring and finally let herself in with the latch key Dick had provided for her. There was nothing to do but wait; that she knew. But she also knew she couldn't wait patiently. She had been through this so often before!

A full hour must have passed before the telephone started to ring. For a moment Nita thought of not answering it—but then remembered it could be Dick calling, though such a possibility was one in a thousand.

"Nita?" a girl's voice said, recognizing her greeting. "This is Lona Kirkpatrick." The young pretty wife of Police Commissioner Stanley Kirkpatrick sounded worried, almost hesitant to give the reason for her call. "Darling," she went on, "I just had to call. It's all so foolish, I suppose just some joke, probably, and doesn't mean a thing..."

Nita laughed. "For goodness sake, Lona! Tell me."

"Well, Stanley received a tip tonight and he seemed very excited about it—as he always is. Someone called to say that they would..." Lona Kirkpatrick's words trailed off. After a brief pause, as though bracing herself against the message she had to give, her voice strained, she said quickly, bluntly, "Nita, they've set a trap for the *Spider*! That's what Stan was so excited about tonight—and this time the trap worked. Nita, darling, this time they've caught the *Spider*!"

A long moment of silence followed. Nita could sense Lona's anguish at being the one to pass on such news; she could see her standing rigidly with the phone tight-held in a white-knuckled hand. Neither girl spoke for a time, and it was Lona who picked up the conversation again.

"It seems impossible—but I'm afraid it's true," she went on, her voice low. "A friend of Stan's

and mine who is an official at headquarters called me a minute ago. He told me an official report had just come in. The *Spider* is in the hands of the police."

The first shock of the news was gone now. Nita's great love for Dick, her gnawing fear that such a thing as this might happen, had momentarily blinded her faith in Dick's clever resourcefulness. The *Spider* trapped? Impossible! That's the way Nita had to believe. She wouldn't accept any other possibility.

A little laugh came from her throat. "Lona, dear, someone blundered—but it wasn't the *Spider*. The mistake was made by whomever it was that sent in that false report. Believe me— and don't take this to heart. You'll see."

But after she had hung up, Nita van Sloan wasn't able herself to adopt the advice she had given Lona Kirkpatrick. Like the eternally menacing sword of Damocles, over her hung the threat of that awful day in the future when Dick could set out on his last adventure—and not return. Could this be it? Was the case-book of the *Spider* finally to be marked closed?

Nita mixed herself a highball over at the portable bar, but left it standing there untasted. She lit a cigarette and it burned itself to a long gray ash, unnoticed in the tray on the coffee table. Finally Nita went out onto the terrace of Dick's penthouse and stood there in the cool night, the city a twinkling plaything at her feet, her mind far from the lovely scene she gazed down upon.

The urgent ringing of the telephone brought Nita quickly back into the living room. This might be Dick calling her now! She swept up the telephone, said abruptly:

"Nita van Sloan speaking. Who is this, please?"

But the voice on the other end wasn't Dick's. It was a heavy, muffled voice; one that was apparently disguised.

"Miss van Sloan? I thought you might be concerned about the welfare of your good friend, Richard Wentworth. It seems he got himself in a little jam tonight—one that will prove fatal unless you're willing to help him. Now, shall I continue?"

Nita tensed. Caution was with her now. She would never admit that Richard Wentworth and the *Spider* were one and the same. It was her most closely guarded secret. Certainly this caller hadn't suggested as much, but his call coming on the heels of Lona's rang an alarm in Nita's mind.

"Will you please be more specific?" she asked. Mr. Wentworth isn't the type of man who customarily needs help. He can well take care of himself. However, I am certainly willing to do what I can for him."

"Because of the circumstances," the voice said smoothly, "I can't give you my name at the moment. And the things I have to say would best be spoken in private, not over this wire. So if you want to hear more you must call in person at 72 Brown Street, in Greenwich Village. Just ring the bell of the apartment on the second floor, rear.

We'll be waiting."

Nita was thoughtful for a moment after she hung up. She knew Brown Street to be a particularly poor section of the slums. That, of itself, pointed to danger even without the attendant circumstances. She completely distrusted the call. But if Dick was in trouble and by now Nita had to admit reluctantly that he undoubtedly was, for otherwise he would have gotten in touch with her—if Dick was in trouble, the best way she could serve him would be to walk into this present trap willingly. By being near him, she might be able to serve.

Nita picked up the handbag she had been carrying earlier that night and opened it to make sure her small, nickled automatic was still there. Then she quickly put on her hat and coat.

Only minutes after that last call Nita opened the front door and left the penthouse apartment, willingly walking into a trap to be by Dick's side.

Rather than go directly to the Brown Street address, Nita parked the big Daimler some blocks away and decided to do some reconnoitering beforehand. The section gave an even worse appearance than she had remembered it. Moldering, dilapidated buildings lined the narrow, crooked streets; half the houses were condemned, their boarded-up windows staring down on the passerby like blind, sightless eyes. This was the domain of poverty and filth, the breeding-place of crime.

It was a block above Brown Street that Nita van Sloan heard her name called by someone behind her. She turned, wondering, for the voice sounded vaguely familiar. Then the man was striding up to her, his body almost a caricature of a human being. Exaggeratedly tall, he must have measured close to seven feet. His large head set atop a painfully thin frame, and his wide-staring eyes looked at her with a burning, blazing intensity. He was undoubtedly a fanatic— and it was then Nita remembered him. He was Silas Breen, the rabid reformer who constantly harangued the public for its sins, shouting from the platforms of the halls he hired.

"You're Miss van Sloan,"—he began abruptly in a tense, hard voice. "I've seen your picture in the papers. I've often envied you your position and influence, because of the good you could do. Just imagine what..."

"Please," Nita interrupted him, not unkindly. "I have an important appointment, you see. It's nice that you recognized me, and I'm glad you said hello. But just at the moment..."

"I'm Silas Breen," the tall man stated, as though anxious she should know who he was, his pride sounding in his tone. "And— oh, yes— something else important. I called to you because I absolutely have to get in touch with Richard Wentworth right away. It's desperately urgent. I thought you might know where he can be found at the moment."

"Not just now," Nita said. ''But I can leave a message for him. He can call you tomorrow, by phone. Perhaps..."

"Not tomorrow!" Breen almost shouted, waving his fantastically long arms. "Tonight! You see, I have certain definite information that may lead to a solution of this present horrible crime wave. As you know, I have many contacts with the underworld, due to my criminal-rehabilitation program. This information, placed in the hands of a man with contacts, resourcefulness and courage may be the only means of saving many human lives. Perhaps hundreds of them! Now do you understand?"

"I still can't help you," Nita told him. "I'm sorry." She started to turn away, anxious to get to Dick's side, but the reformer grasped her arm urgently.

"Listen!" he urged. "One of the focal points of this whole underworld campaign is in a little, obscure bar not far from where we stand now. It's called the East Side Bar. If you can't locate Richard Wentworth for me, I'm going there alone! I can't let more innocent people be killed! I can't stand by!"

At the name of the East Side Bar Nita had suddenly stiffened. That was the very place Dick had been headed for earlier, in the character of Blinky McQuade! She knew what a desperately dangerous hide-out it was-and here this crack-pot, harmless reformer was threatening to invade that den alone! He wouldn't last in that place for five minutes!

"Please!" she asked urgently.

"Don't do a thing until you've talked to Mr. Wentworth! Believe me, it could be suicidal and your information would then prove of value to no one. Within an hour or two Mr. Wentworth will call on you himself."

"I can't wait," Silas Breen said stubbornly. "I'm going there right now! Silas Breen crusades for the people—the simple, God-fearing and innocent!"

"I not only warn you," Nita tried again, "I beg you not to go to that place alone."

The last of her words were spoken to Silas Breen's retreating back. He was already striding away on what he probably thought was another crusade against crime. It might be another crusade, all right, but it would probably be his last.

Helpless in the face of the man's persistence, Nita shrugged and turned away. She had urgent work of her own to do, and now her steps were more rapid as she approached Brown Street. She had wasted too much time as it was.

As she turned the corner, Nita had a strange experience. A taxi cab swung about the corner, too, going in the opposite direction, and as it flashed under the street lamp Nita could have sworn that she saw Dick sitting tensely in the rear seat. So complete was her momentary conviction in that first second that she involuntarily came to a halt and turned to stare after the cab. But reason told her immediately afterward that she had been mistaken.

If Dick were free enough to go riding about in cabs, she realized, he would certainly be free enough to telephone her—and he would not have failed to do so an hour or more ago. It was simply that her fear for Dick's safety was so great that she wanted to see him safe and at liberty.

She shrugged away the strange feeling that had come over her and hurried on, a moment later coming to number 72, an ancient and crumbling tenement. Without hesitation, she ran up the stoop and entered the dingy hallway.

Caution came to Nita as she mounted the stairs. She took the automatic from her handbag and carried it concealed in the pocket of her sports coat. She knew the traps that could be laid in this dim, gas-lighted hallway. She wouldn't be taken unaware.

Second floor, rear; those were her instructions. The nameplate on the door bore no name when she came to it, but she pushed the bell and stood back out of arm's reach from the door. A soft chiming sounded within, in answer to her ring, and the strangeness of hearing it in this cold-water tenement house surprised Nita—a surprise that grew even greater when the door finally opened.

A man stood before her, eyebrows raised inquiringly, and the butler's uniform he ware grossly misfit him. Cut obviously for a far larger man, it hung in folds on his body, while the trouser and sleeve cuffs had been turned back generously to allow unimpeded use of the limbs. A butler in a house like this!

Nita's shock when she got inside was as great as Dick Wentworth's when he had viewed it earlier that evening. The strangely mixed furniture, combined with the expensiveness of the furnishings, struck Nita immediately. Her distrust, her sense of danger, was even greater now than before.

"May I know whose home this is?" Nita asked, venturing into the foyer only just past the threshold.

The door closed with a clunk behind her, its sound ominous.

The butler twisted his face into what was supposed to be a grin. He pointed to his mouth and throat, shaking his head, which indicated that he was dumb, unable to speak. Then he made a gesture toward the living room beyond. It was quiet in there, indirect lighting illuminating the entire room. Nita nodded her head and advanced slowly, cautiously, toward the doorway.

The automatic, gripped tight in Nita's fist, was trained steadily ahead of her, the pocket of her coat hiding it from view. Her tension relaxed somewhat, however, when she had entered the room. At first glance it seemed to be empty.

After a second, Nita van Sloan saw the beefy man across the room. Perhaps, had he been glaring at her murderously, or had he been aiming a gun in her direction, Nita would have felt less alarm than at his actual reception of her. His face was beaded with sweat, the veins of his forehead bulging, and in his eyes was a look of desperate, haunting terror.

He was looking at Nita as though she had come to assassinate him! He appeared to be gazing on his merciless executioner!

"He looks upon his murderer," a quiet voice behind Nita said. "Not a pretty sight, is he? Neither is murder!"

Nita had begun to whirl at the first sound. As she did so, she realized the thick Oriental carpet had muffled any slightest sound of footfalls-and that she should have remained constantly with the wall directly at her back to prevent the very trap she had fallen into.

Her spin half completed, Nita felt strong hands grip her by the shoulders, felt a second pair of hands seize her arms and pinion them to her sides. Automatically, she had ripped the gun from her pocket, but she had not been fast enough, since it was necessary for her to turn before she could fire. Now the automatic was torn from her grasp and she was left defenseless.

The ludicrously garbed butler came through a door on the far side of the room and approached Nita. Someone behind her, someone she was prevented from seeing, handed the gun to the butler.

Nita's own breathing was loud in her ears as She continued to struggle, hopeless though the odds were.

"Let Big Bill have it," that same quiet voice directed. "Speed him on his way. His usefulness to us is finished."

Big Bill—whom Nita recognized now as a shady politician with criminal leanings, began to squirm and writhe even more frantically as the butler walked purposefully toward him. It was then that Nita saw he was bound to the armchair, hand and foot, and that a wire gag had been thrust into his mouth. And she realized, too, what the leader's orders had meant.

"No! You can't!" she cried out, realizing only that it was a helpless human being she saw across the room in that chair. "None of you could possibly be so cold-blooded as to..."

The rest of her words were drowned out by the sound of the gun. Deliberately and without haste the butler walked up to the writhing Big Bill, calmly raised the gun and methodically emptied its eight slugs into the beefy politician's chest. Big Bill was dead long before the last slug had ripped into his body.

Nita had ceased to struggle now. She realized how futile such attempts were—just as she understood the type of men into whose hands she had been lured. Cold, emotionless killers. Men who made a profitable business of murder. Experts in the art of human slaughter.

The girl Richard Wentworth loved—the girl who had loyally and fearlessly come to him when she thought him trapped—watched a second gunman untie Big Bill's corpse, remove the gag and roll his limp body onto the rug before his blood had seeped through his clothing and onto the fabric of the chair.

Meantime, the thug in the butler's uniform picked up Nita's handbag from where it had fallen. After emptying its contents onto the rug, he went about simulating the evidence of a struggle in the room: overturning a chair and table; smashing a vase; scuffing and wrinkling the carpet.

Nita didn't realize the chloroformed cloth was coming until a hand from behind had actually pressed it over her mouth and nose. With her first breath the fumes warned her. Instinctively, she tried to hold her breath. By the time her pulses were drumming and pounding in her temples she knew how useless it was. To remain alive she had to breathe, while the fumes she must breathe meant only unconsciousness—death!

"Everything's set, chief," a voice behind her said.

Now the room was beginning slowly to revolve before Nita's eyes.

"Splendid!" the soft-spoken man replied. "This is one fix Wentworth won't be able to get out of. Maybe one of you had better call the police. They can pick up his sweetheart for murder—and after that the fool Wentworth will play the tune our way—or else!"

The room was blacking out. Nita fought against the blackness, but it was useless. Everything faded as a loud humming sounded monotonously in her ears. Nita van Sloan was out cold.

6

HOPELESS SEARCH

WHEN Richard Wentworth stepped quickly from the elevator into his private penthouse hallway, the faithful Ram Singh was standing with the front door of the apartment held open. The thicket of black beard that grew almost to his eyes was in violent contrast with the Sikh's white silk, tight-bound turban. Those dark eyes of his were worried now to a point of physical pain—but behind that worry there showed a cold, terrible anger. Ram Singh loved his missie sahib—and awful would be the violent end of any man who dared to harm her.

"There is no further news, sahib?" he asked Wentworth in his deep-chested, booming voice. "Have you learned anything more of the missie sahib?" The door swung fully open.

Richard Wentworth hadn't the heart to speak; he simply shook his head and walked on into the living room, where Ram Singh followed him. Ram Singh's terribly powerful body was obviously at hair-trigger readiness to spring into action on Wentworth's order, but now the giant of a man stood patiently at one end of the room, waiting for his master to speak. Dick Wentworth paced twice up and down the length of the room.

Suddenly he swung to face Ram Singh, his arms held wide in a gesture of momentary frustration. "What can we do, Ram Singh? What on earth can a man do with a problem like this? Just look at the facts that face us:

"The missie sahib is missing, somewhere in this city of seven million persons. We don't know where to start looking—east, west, uptown or downtown."

"Could there still be some happy solution?" Ram Singh asked, though the negative answer to his own question was apparent in his doleful tone. "The home of friends perhaps shelter her. Or maybe some unexpected duty..."

Wentworth shook his head. "The missie sahib said she'd wait here for me until my return. Nothing but an extremely urgent matter could have called her away—and even then she'd have left a note for me with either you or Jackson. Her leaving as she did suggests that she may have been seized and carried away by force which obviously couldn't have happened. Either that, or—" and Richard Wentworth suddenly snapped his fingers, their crack loud in the room— "either that, or she thought she was going to meet me at the end of the trip! You see, Ram Singh? If she were on her way to meet me, any note or message would obviously be unnecessary! There's the answer. She was fooled somehow, tricked!"

A restrained rumble sounded deep in the Sikh's throat. "And your orders to me, sahib? One waits but to obey."

Richard Wentworth was thinking quickly. The answer as to how Nita had been lured outside didn't lessen his problem any. It made it more urgent, if anything, for now he realized the desperate urgency of Nita's plight.

"Here are your orders," Wentworth snapped suddenly, and the huge servant tensed expectantly. "Three times tonight I have experienced danger—and always in the same section of the city. The lower east side! There's more than coincidence in that. So you, Ram

Singh, go to the lower east side and search. Search! The missie sahib must be found, and at once!

"Perhaps you will see someone you recognize, spot a familiar car—perhaps even discover the Daimler parked on a street. Such a lead would narrow our search, so look well, Ram Singh."

The Sikh rumbled his assent, took a step toward the door before he stopped abruptly. "And you, sahib, you take another course? You have a second plan?"

Richard Wentworth nodded, his face unnaturally white, his expression grim. He took a deep breath. "There's one other way, Ram Singh, and with Nita in danger, I must take it. I'm going to Police Commissioner Kirkpatrick's home. I'll have to ask his aid, tell him Nita's missing under menacing circumstances. I'll have to ask his help in sending out a general alarm to all patrol cars. It's the only other way.

"But one other thing, Ram Singh. If you get any clue, no matter how seemingly vague, as to the missie sahib's whereabouts, get in touch with me immediately either at the Commissioner's or here at home. And do you know the Hotel Madden, that four-bit flophouse over on the east side?"

Ram Singh nodded wordlessly, his expression intent.

"Good. Then hire one of the loafers in the lobby to take any messages for you that come through on the public phone in the lobby. There's only one such booth and you can easily find one of those down-and-outs who'll sit up all night for a dollar. You can stop by the Madden at odd intervals to see if any message has come through from me. I may have further orders."

Ram Singh salaamed, lifting his cupped hands to his forehead in submission. "I hear and obey," he intoned.

Richard Wentworth swung about to face Jackson, who had come silently into the room and now stood stiffly at attention, the ex-soldier shoving plainly in his bearing. "I'm ready, Major," he said briskly. Then, a look almost of pleading coming into his expression, he added plaintively, "Boss, I'm in on this, too, ain't I? You've got a small assignment for the old sergeant, huh?"

"I have, and an extremely important one," Wentworth snapped, already on his way to the door. Jackson trailed at his heels. "I want you to sit on top of that phone until I get back! You know where I'll be—and Nita might just possibly find some way of calling in. Furthermore, Kirkpatrick will suspect plenty after I've told him about Nita— and with the developments that may come up tonight, all of us will need an alibi. Kirkpatrick must be kept away from the apartment until we're all safely back!"

The slamming of the front door punctuated the last word of his sentence. Richard Wentworth had started on his desperate adventure, prepared at any moment to become the feared and fearsome *Spider* if that guise could assist in the return of the girl he loved...

Commissioner Stanley Kirkpatrick put aside the book he had been reading and came to his feet as his manservant ushered Dick Wentworth into the room. His trim military mustache and erect bearing were the same as ever, but there was something in his greeting that hinted at a certain restraint. The bitter fact that the *Spider* had eluded him again was only made more irritating by the added fact that the *Spider* had also taunted his whole police force in doing so. Kirkpatrick was a smart, clever man; those who served under him were capable and trained. And the Commissioner hated to have them all duped as though they were fools.

"Well, Dick! Good evening," he said. "You find me a bachelor again—temporarily. Lona has gone to a dinner party and some sort of affair afterward. As a matter of fact, I was invited too, of course. Thought I'd have rather a pleasant time." He looked sharply at the younger man. Unfortunately, a sudden emergency down at headquarters forced me to cancel my plans at the last moment, though you may know more about that than I."

Dick tried to force a laugh, which was the way he always greeted the Commissioner's well-founded but unprovable accusations, but tonight he wasn't very successful. His heart was heavy and a grim fear occupied his mind. Stanley Kirkpatrick must have noticed it; then he must have seen the pale, drawn look about Wentworth's face. Then next he spoke, his tone had changed. Solicitude for his friend was plain in his voice.

. "Dick, old man! What's the trouble? You're not your old self, my boy. Just what's troubling you? Anything I could help you solve? Ask anything of me. "

"There is something you could do. A whole lot," Wentworth told him slowly. "But, somehow, it's difficult to ask."

"Wentworth stopped then and Kirkpatrick didn't urge him on; he let Dick take his time. Reaching for a pipe on the table beside him, pulling a tobacco humidor close, he began to charge his pipe. At last, in a quiet voice and obviously engrossed in the serious business of acquiring an even, smooth-burning glow in the bowl, he murmured almost to himself:

"There's only one thing in this whole world that could upset you this much, Dick. Personally, you fear nothing—yet you're actually pale. That means but one thing. Danger or disaster threatens someone you love dearly. Nita."

Somehow that made it much easier for Dick. "That's it. Nita," he replied, glad that his old friend had understood so readily. "She's in desperate trouble, Kirk, of that I'm convinced. The devil of it is, I don't know where she could be or exactly who is threatening her. It could be anywhere, anyone. But she's suddenly disappeared; that much I know. And I have reason to suspect that the focal point of the underworld threat will be found down on the lower east side."

Commissioner Kirkpatrick looked up sharply, once again the efficient, aggressive police officer. "Underworld threat? Are you trying to tell me, Dick, that Nita has somehow gotten herself involved with criminals? Furthermore, you mention the lower east side as a positive location. May I inquire just why you have reason to suspect that section of town?"

"Please, Kirk." The sincerity of Richard Wentworth's tone was unmistakable; his suffering was obvious. "For just this once, take my word for it without demanding explanations. Sound a general alarm for a missing person and add a suspicion-of-violence tag. Kirk, I've got to find Nita without delay!"

Surprisingly, Kirkpatrick, Commissioner of Police for New York City, seemed to temporize between friendship and duty. "You said you had reason to suspect; and suspicion isn't proof of knowledge. As a matter of fact, the lower east side of the city is a logical section in which to look for violence. So let my questions pass. I'll put through a call to headquarters on the private line. We'll have your Nita back in no time."

Relief flooded through Wentworth as he saw Kirkpatrick get up and stride into his library and open his official line direct to headquarters. In his anxiety, Dick had followed him to the threshold, stood there listening as he heard the orders rapped out. In a matter of moments now that alarm would be sounding in every police patrol car in the city.

Stanley Kirkpatrick had hung up and turned toward the door when the phone ringed, indicating a headquarters call direct to the commissioner himself. Kirkpatrick's words were enough to give Wentworth the gist of the incoming message.

Murdered? Well, I can't say it's any great loss to humanity, but the act is still a capital offense. I don't like that anonymous stuff, though. We'll investigate immediately, of course. Now, what about location. Was that given too?....72 Brown! Why that's where he lived. Go on, man. What else?.... A girl? This begins to sound like the real thing. Call out a dozen squad cars and send them down there flying! I'll be along and join you as soon as possible. Make this fast!

If we can pick her up before she gets out of the section, the case is sewed up! Throw a cordon around the Brown Street section and don't let so much as a cat get through!"

At the mention of the address, Richard Wentworth stiffened, as though from an electric shock. That was Big Bill Dwyer's home. Then, as the Commissioner's excitement mounted, Wentworth's soared far beyond. Brown Street! The lower east side! A murder! A girl obviously accused anonymously, undoubtedly trapped at or near the scene of the crimes They where obviously talking about Nita, though she was unidentified as yet—and she had been framed for murder!

Sweat beaded on Richard Wentworth's hands and forehead. Nita's only chance now was for him to reach her and spirit her away before the police reached that address! But how could he possibly hope to out distance those flying squad cars with their howling sirens? There could be but one way—through Ram Singh, warned by telephone! Ram Singh was his only hope!

Commissioner Kirkpatrick came back into the living room fast. This emergency had made him once again the coldly precise police official. As yet, he hadn't connected Nita van Sloan with the idea of murder. Who would? But once he had time to recall Wentworth's mention of the lower east side, the fact that Nita was his concern, he'd immediately put two and two together.

With a remark in passing, he hurried on into the rear of the apartment, headed for his bedroom. Once he was out of sight, Dick was at the regular telephone in a bound. His finger jabbed out the dial number of the Hotel Madden and after what seemed an eternity a slow, sleepy voice answered. As luck would have it, Ram Singh wasn't there but he'd be back soon. Soon! With seconds precious as the police cars roared to the scene, Wentworth had prayed for a break of luck. It hadn't worked.

Swiftly, in a soft yet distinct voice, he gave out his orders as simply as possible. To Wentworth, the man on the other end seemed a moron. Could he get the instructions right, be trusted to pass them on accurately? To make sure, he started to repeat his orders but Kirkpatrick's footfalls approaching along the hall made him hang up abruptly. Even the small bit of luck that would have meant another minute's talking time wasn't given him. Everything— perhaps even Nita's life—now depended on the brain and memory of the man who had taken the message for Ram Singh. And that meant a disinterested stranger—probably a waterfront bum!

''Have an emergency call, Dick," Kirkpatrick told him quickly. "Like to come along? It promises to be exciting."

"Might as well, Kirk," he forced his lips to drawl—but what a different emotion was in his heart!

During the ride in the Commissioner's official car, Wentworth's hands, fisted in the pockets of his topcoat, clenched until his nails dug into his palms. The four motorcycles ahead, screaming for a clear road, told him too clearly how efficient was the police force he now found himself pitted against. And the roar of the powerful motor of the limousine kept repeating a single agonizing question in his ears: "Did Ran Singh get the message; will he be in time? Did Ram Singh get the message; will he be in time?" And his heart repeated a single word in answer to each repeated question: "Nita! Nita!"

As they pierced swiftly, deeper and deeper into the lower part of the city, the faint wailing of far-off sirens could be heard. The banshee wails seemed to come from every direction—all converging on Brown Street.

When the Police Commissioner's limousine was about six blocks from their destination, Richard Wentworth heard the motorcycles ahead suddenly scream their sirens into a higher, earsplitting key— and then both he and the Commissioner were thrown violently forward as the uniformed chauffeur slammed down on the brakes sending the car into a skid.

At rest finally, the heavy car still rocking from the strain, the motorcycles ahead now up on the sidewalk, forced there by the obstruction—the two of them leaped to peer out of the windows. Ahead they saw tow automobiles savagely interlocked from their smash, one of them lying on its side. A truck, evidently unable to avoid the smash-up, had ploughed into the mass, increasing the accidental barricade of the street.

Cursing under his breath, Commissioner Kirkpatrick took time out to roar at the driver to put the car about and try another approach. But it was difficult to turn the long car in that narrow side street; precious minutes were lost before they were under way again.

A second time they found the way blocked— this time, apparently, by a fire. Hook-and-ladders and chemical engines very completely jammed the street—and they had the authority to do so. Almost bursting, Stanley Kirkpatrick forced his shaking voice to be calm as he ordered another detour.

Inside, Richard Wentworth glowed with happiness. His luck was breaking at last. A simple accident—one that could happen anywhere, anytime had been further complicated by that everyday occurrence, a fire. Two small offerings by fate, both happening at the same time and in the same section—but how much they meant to two people who loved each other.

But on the third block they tried, Wentworth's previous joy fizzled and died abruptly. The knowledge of disaster swept all other emotions aside, leaving only despair. Ram Singh was there, just ahead! Blocks from Nita, Ram Singh fought like a wild man, a man possessed of demons and he fought for his very life!

Police cars jammed the street; blue-coats were everywhere; guns were blazing; the surrounding houses showed cops lining the balustrades on the roofs, guns drawn; a dozen or more searchlights blazed up into the darkness and all where focused on the same object—on Ram Singh, the embattled giant and roaring warrior!

Wentworth's desperate glance took the situation in immediately. Atop one building, crouching behind a brick chimney, was his faithful Sikh servant. Facing him, but also concealed, were a score of police, their guns cracking viciously. Ram Singh's two big guns snapped back—whining lead in every direction but his battle was obviously hopeless. Deliberately avoiding wounding any of his antagonists, the black-bearded man would soon be rushed and physically overpowered by several score of husky police. And he had no way of retreat. A second, taller building placed a blank wall at his back, a wall that not even a cat could have climbed.

Wentworth found himself outside with the gathering crowd now, though he didn't remember leaving the car. He groaned aloud in the din of noise that shattered the night. Ram Singh still blocks away from Brown Street and Nita, surrounded, trapped.

That could mean but one thing. The desperate attempt of Richard Wentworth and Ram Singh had failed utterly—and now the faithful servant was going do down gloriously in their defeat, perhaps paying for his act with his very life!

7

RAM SINGH AT BAY!

HEN Ram Singh had reached the lower east side earlier that evening, following his master's instructions, his first act had been to stalk to the Hotel Madden, his giant strides carrying him there at what would have been a trotting gait for the ordinary man. He had to arrange for the reception of telephoned messages, should sudden new instructions come through.

The lobby was as Richard Wentworth had described it: shabby, dusty, threadbare, its uncarpeted tile floor begrimed by the shuffling passage of many dispirited feet. The occupants of the lobby there in perfect harmony with their surroundings. As he examined the dozen or more guests who slouched in the armchairs, Ram Singh frowned with distaste. Nor was it poverty that he frowned upon; that he could sympathize with, understand. It was the dissolute living and shiftless characters of these men that caused his disapproval.

One of the occupants, a younger man and the most likely looking of the lot, Ram Singh selected as his agent. The transaction was quickly made. All incoming messages on the public phone were to be taken by him; any messages for Ram Singh were to be written down. Then the Sikh tore a five-dollar bill in half, passing part of it to the other and promising the matching half when the night's work was done.

Out on the street again, Ram Singh's seemingly hopeless task began. Striding through the night, his towering form must have seemed an apparition from another world to those few startled pedestrians he passed. But he hadn't eyes for their amazed stares, their sudden and abrupt change of course. A glance at each face showed them to be strangers and he pressed doggedly on.

After perhaps half an hour of prowling, Ram Singh returned to the Madden. There was nothing for him by phone. The Sikh had an uncanny sense of approaching disaster, and that sense began to trouble him now, try though he did to throw it off. Was his missie sahib's hour fast approaching? Was she trying to get some message through to him? The massive Sikh made a whining sound in his throat and the length of his strides increased.

Suddenly, on a dim side street, he slammed to an abrupt halt, a great breath bellowing into his lungs. He wheeled and strode across the narrow avenue. No, he had not been mistaken! There, parked at the curb where she had left it, was the big Daimler car of Wentworth's that Nita had borrowed earlier that night! Now, he was really getting close to his missie sahib, and this news must be quickly relayed to the sahib.

First, though, Ram Singh swung open the front door of the car. The ignition keys were gone, of course, but he knew where a second set were always kept hidden. These he pocketed, should their emergency use become necessary.

Now trotting lightly and easily, he sped back to the Madden, which promised the nearest telephone in that section. As he came into the lobby, though, his message-boy came quickly to his feet, thrusting a piece of paper forward. This he scanned quickly, read again more carefully, and a rumble sounded in his chest at the grim meaning of the words.

Tell Ram Singh that the one he seeks is at 72 Brown Street, in the apartment of Big Bill Dwyer. She is in desperate danger. Even now the

*police are on their way. She must be safely removed. But at all costs
the police must be prevented from getting there first. At all costs!*

Ram Singh passed over the second half of the five-dollar bill and
then one of his huge hands reached out to grasp the messenger by
his shoulder, all but lifting him from his feet as it rocked him slowly,
emphatically back and forth.

"One is not troubled with the loose tongue of an old woman?"
he rumbled. "If so, it is well to remember that life is sweet; death
bitter and swift!"

His blazing eyes burned into the other's, and the down-and-outer
turned deathly white at what he saw there. He tried to speak but no
words would come from his lips. Then, almost before he was aware
of the action, Ram Singh had spun on his heel and strode from the
lobby.

Out in the street again, Ram Singh was about to break into a run
to cross the ten blocks that separated him from his missie sahib but
something caused him to snap stiffly erect, his head thrown back
and tilted slightly to one side. No, he had not been mistaken! Far in
the distance, his supremely acute hearing had picked up the barest
whisper of a sound. Police sirens! Already they were on their way!
It would be impossible to outrun them on foot!

In that moment of extreme crisis, Ram Singh's brain worked
furiously. After but a second's hesitation, he knew what he must
do— and then he was speeding down the dark street.

At the corner he skidded to a halt, jumped to the red-painted fire-
alarm box there and deliberately twisted the alarm handle furiously
back and forth! Then he was away again. Behind him a policeman's
whistle shrilled a warning to stop—and, after a moment, Ram Singh
did. But by that time he was again before a red-painted box on
the far corner. Careless of the fact that he stood directly beneath a
revealing street lamp, he again sent in his urgent alarm! Those who
saw him must have thought him a madman.

But Ram Singh wasn't satisfied with that. He knew the location of the East Side Bar—Blinky McQuade's underworld hangout—and toward that unsavory place he raced, turning in two more fire alarms on the way. Already he could hear the deep-throated booming of the fire apparatus mingling with the shriller police sirens and the urgently staccato bells. A mild, fierce grin creased his face now as he burst through the doors of the bar and stood in the middle of the suddenly quiet room, arms akimbo set. To greet the silence he threw back his turbaned, thick-bearded head and gave forth a mighty bellow of laughter that reverberated through the room. His eyes gleamed with an unholy brightness as he looked about the evil-faced crowd that faced him.

Deliberately selecting the biggest man present—an ox-like hulk of a man who stood at the bar with a glass of beer in front of him—Ram Singh walked over to face him.

"Is the beer suddenly bitter, dog?' he rumbled, one hand picking up the glass. "Here, drink!" And Ram Singh hurled the full contents of the glass directly into the plug-ugly's face!

Roaring riot followed instantly. A backhanded slap of Ram Singh's huge hand knocked the beer-blinded thug from his path and a single bound had carried him across the bar, where he landed lightly beside the startled bartender. A twist and heave of the Sikh's mighty arms and the bartender was flying bodily from behind this temporary barricade. Three seated customers caught the force of the man's weight and the whole group crashed backward in a twisting tangle onto the sawdust-strewn floor.

A hurtling chair soared toward Ram Singh's head, but the Sikh lithely hopped to one side. The chair rocketed into the large mirror behind him and a crashing shower of glass spewed over the bar. Almost immediately, Ram Singh went into further action. A tremendous battle-cry welling from his massive chest, the wild grin of battle slicing his features ferociously to reveal his pearl-white teeth, he began seizing and hurling the bottles that lined the back of the bar. They smashed into every corner of the room, and each time Ram Singh had sent one whizzing toward a target he'd duck back beneath his barricade, only to re-appear at another point a split second later.

The obvious happened a moment or too later. One of the thug customers opened up with a gun, its sharp blasting punctuating the chaotic bedlam of splintering glass, screamed epithets, raging shouts, crashing furniture and the Sikh's joyous, thunderous battle song. All hell had truly broken loose.

Other guns joined that first one—but Ram Singh was well protected and an elusive target. For a second his head and shoulders would appear. At one point his arm would flail forward, a bottle would hurtle viciously at an unprotected head, guns could blast out a volley—and at the same instant, Ram Singh would be gone. Behind him, bottles could seem to leap into the air and dissolve in a shower of glass and whiskey as the lead slugs sang into them— but by that time their human target would be yards away.

It's probable some personal feuds were settled at that opportune time. Certain it is that not all the slugs came Ram Singh's way—and that several customers were wounded by more lethal ammunition than Ram Singh's bottle barrage. But the shooting was exactly what the Sikh wanted— and after several minutes he knew that his stratagem had been successful. Close by, his ears picked up the sound of approaching riot-squad cars.

Suddenly Ram Singh was no longer behind the bar. A mighty leap had carried him half way into the rear room, and before anyone was fully aware, he was gone. The riot continued, however—and that, too, was what Ram Singh wanted.

Into the back alley leading from the place he darted—and saw two dark forms writhing their way to freedom through a narrow window. One of the men saw him at the same moment, and blasted a shot at Ram Singh without warning or reason. The bullet seared the Sikh's arm, bringing a roar of rage from him.

"Stop, dogs, and fight!" he thundered. "Fight with your pop-guns, two to one, and I'll slit your yellow bellies!"

The two men raced into the street, Ram Singh on their heels, but their method of escape was perfect. By the time Ram Singh had reached the sidewalk, they were in their car—a heavy black sedan-roaring into high gear.

A large crowd of curious onlookers had gathered now, along with the police, though they stood well out of range of stray bullets. The mob did jam the street completely, though, and that was what the Sikh wanted. He grinned with satisfaction.

Someone in the crowd was shouting to the police and pointing toward Ram Singh, so he broke into a run as police bullets came singing after him, whining close in the darkness. Other footsteps pounded behind him, and he knew capture seemed imminent. Then a sudden thought struck him. The Daimler! It was parked but a few short blocks away.

Once in the car. Ram Singh quickly eluded his pursuers for a few precious moments. And he still had work to do. His sahib had said that the police must not reach the apartment in which the missie sahib was trapped—and at all costs! Ram Singh grinned without humor. The police would never reach her, not if it took ten inspired riots to jam up the section so thoroughly that not even the Commissioner himself could get through!

Ram Singh hadn't decided his next move as he sent the Daimler speeding through the night. One more incident to congest the section even further and he'd be ready to fight his way to the missie sahib's side. But what could he do that he hadn't already done? And the answer came immediately.

Ram Singh was approaching an intersection just then, and as he was about to cross, a second car came roaring down the side street, its horn blaring imperiously, and cut directly across the nose of Ram Singh's Daimler. He had to slap on his brakes hard to avoid a smash-up—and it was only after the other car had passed that he recognized it unquestionably. It was the black sedan the gunmen had used in their get-away a few minutes ago!

The deep-throated roar of the Daimler's powerful engine grew louder as Ram Singh gave it the gun; the needle on the speed gauge

mounted until it was up past sixty on the turns of those narrow streets, the tires whinnied in protest. But Ram Singh had his plan. He cut over one block, then paralleled the course of the gangster's car, trying to overtake them. Four blocks later he cut back again to the original avenue, skidded to a halt and sent an anxious glance in the direction from which they should be approaching. The gleam of their headlights made him grunt with satisfaction. They were still half a block away, coming fast.

As they entered the intersection, Ram Singh deliberately nosed the Daimler directly into their path. Again that imperious horn but this time it got no response. A wild screaming of braked tires followed as the second car tried to stop, but it was hopeless. Then the driver swung his wheel desperately, jolted up onto the sidewalk in an attempt to cut behind the Sikh's car. It looked for a moment as though he'd make it, but Ram Singh was quick too. He snapped the Daimler into reverse, let the clutch snap out—and plunged backward into the side of the wildly slewing gangster car, his motor wide open!

The shattering crash of rending metal boomed loudly; the tinkling sound of broken glass sounded almost immediately afterward, mingling with the sharp hissing of a punctured tire. But Ram Singh didn't stop there. He left his powerful motor wide open, and slowly the other car, heavy though it was, heeled over sideways, teetered uncertainly for a moment, and finally crashed onto its side like a monster mortally wounded. A second tire let go then, this time with an explosive report.

No sooner had the other car crashed onto its side than Ram Singh was out of the Daimler in a bound. Another leap and he was standing high on the side of the capsized vehicle. For a second his hands disappeared into its interior, then reappeared, each one holding a gunman by the scuff of the neck—lifting them out, holding them aloft, with all the ease of a child holding two kittens! Neither man moved; both where unconscious.

Ram Singh looked at them with distaste for a moment, then shook loose the guns from their holsters and dropped one of them back into the car he had been driving, swung the other over and tossed him onto the front seat of the Daimler.

A fast-approaching truck, riding recklessly— without lights, made Ram Singh leap abruptly from the wreck. He had scarcely gained a safe distance when a second shattering crash shook the neighborhood. Now the street was completely blocked by two wrecked cars and an entangled truck. The Sikh knew then the first part of his job was done. The police were effectively blocked off, temporarily, from the Brown Street address. All he had to do now was get to the missie sahib and speed her to safety.

A quick sense of danger warned Ram Singh and his head snapped up, eyes alertly searching. Then he saw them. At one end of the street a group of police were approaching quietly. He had been spotted and this time they weren't taking any chances! A fast glance behind him revealed two prowl cars coasting up silently. He realized that others were just behind these first police and that he was undoubtedly surrounded!

There was only one way of flight left to Ram Singh. Upward! And he took that way, ducking back into the nearest tenement just as the first challenging shout demanded that he surrender— or be shot. He had scarcely gained the entrance foyer before the glass in the door disintegrated under the impact of a bullet.

Racing up the stairs, flight after flight, the Sikh pulled the two big guns from his pockets— the too guns he had taken from the gangsters outside. But even as he reached the roof he knew a bitter sense of defeat. The sahib had forbidden him to shoot policemen— and his only hope would be to shoot his way clear. How else could he get to the missie sahib in time? The roof, he saw at once, was a perfect trap. The only building that adjoined it was a ten-story storehouse, presenting nothing but a blank wall.

Another shot boomed behind Ram Singh then and he knew the first contingent of police had reached the roof.

Jumping to safety behind a brick chimney and snapping back a warning shot to keep his pursuers at bay, Ram Singh heard the approach of more and more patrol cars as the force of police gathered. Searchlights blazed upward to illuminate his crouching form, visible even to those in the street below because of the old-fashioned slanted roof.

A wailing, primeval sort of cry broke from the Sikh's lips. He had failed in his mission! He had failed the sahib and missie sahib! That was all that mattered. Death, to him, meant nothing. And death was coming now, of that he was sure.

Surrounded, without way of retreat, his ammunition limited—and forbidden, anyway, to shoot to kill when the police were involved— he had little doubt of the outcome of the battle.

From the rooftops across the street, guns began to blaze, but these Ram Singh ignored. Until rifles were brought into play, he had little to fear from that direction, especially since the darkness made revolver shooting highly inaccurate. It was only that group that faced him that Ram Singh was concerned about. His guns jumped and barked warning whenever an arm appeared to hurl lead in his direction. But this play was only preliminary; the final disaster would come in a minute or two as soon as reinforcements and tear gas were brought to the rooftop.

Again that wailing cry came from Ram Singh. A tear gas bomb

rolled to his feet spluttering. He seized it, hurled it aside a second followed, a third... The fumes were choking him already and he tried to breathe as little as possible. But his streaming eyes mere half blinded already; he could scarcely see to shoot!

There was something that happened then that made Ram Singh's head snap back, made him summon all his fading resources in a final effort for clear senses. A mighty shout had gone up from the onlookers massed in the street below, a rolling sea of sound, a roar that shuddered and quivered in the night. Ram Singh had heard such a shout before; he had heard it whenever the *Spider* had shown himself before the public. But where could he be now? The faithful Sikh couldn't locate that familiar figure.

It was the brief touch of a silken rope that made Ram Singh look behind him and upward— and there was the *Spider*! That awesome figure stood silhouetted on the balustrade of the storehouse many stories above, his great black cape flowing out behind him in the night wind, his concealing black hat as familiar as death. Like a symbol of the night itself, he stood there as searchlights began to pick out his figure, as guns began to speak viciously.

The silken rope that dangled beside Ram Singh was the *Spider's* web, and Ram Singh didn't have to be told what to do. His powerful arms seized the web, began to haul his body rapidly upward, and as Ram Singh came out from behind his protecting brick chimney, the *Spider*, far above, swung his mounting body from side to side like a pendulum, making him a most difficult target for the guns of the police. Escape lay just above! In exultant cry broke from the Sikh's throat. The *Spider* did not forget his own! The *Spider* himself had come for Ram Singh when disaster had seemed certain!

Then he had reached the roof, Ram Singh felt almost like falling on his knees. "Sahib...!" he began.

"Not now, Ram Singh," the *Spider* ordered tersely—and Ram Singh had rarely heard his voice so grim. "There is less than little time left— and missie sahib nears the final disaster! Come!"

Silently, the two figures fled from the roof. Two phantoms, they must have seemed—one a great-bearded, turbaned giant of a man, the other a black-gowned, full-caped figure that struck some with terror and all with awe ...

8

FLIGHT IN THE NIGHT

ROWN STREET, when they reached it, was still innocent of police cars—but they were on their way. The multiplied confusion Ram Singh had caused should delay the law forces five minutes, perhaps ten—and the startling appearance of the *Spider* had done its part to further the panic of the crowds that now choked the surrounding streets. At best, though, Ram Singh and the *Spider* had only a minute or two in which to work.

It was just as they mounted the steps of number 72 that the first patrol car to break through the cordon of riot could be heard approaching. The emergency urged them to even greater speed, and when they had raced down the length of the second floor hall, the *Spider* hurled his body into the locked door before them. It groaned under the impact, but still held.

Coming fast behind the *Spider*, Ram Singh never even broke his stride. He simply twisted his body side-ways as he hurtled up to the door and the great force of his weight shattered the lock and sent the door crashing inward, twisting drunkenly from one hinge.

Immediately they saw Nita lying there unconscious, the body of the murdered politician sprawled beside her—and then they heard the urgent pounding of feet mounting the stairs. The police had arrived.

The *Spider* was quickly at Nita's side, kneeling to take her in his arms. Nor was Ram Singh idle, waiting for orders; he had understood immediately the meaning of the framed evidence surrounding Nita. He snatched up her automatic, swept up her identifying papers and other articles, stuffed them into his pocket. A second later he was bounding back to the smashed front door of the apartment, barely in time to confront the two uniformed police who came blundering in unsuspectingly.

The sight of the giant, turbaned Sikh was enough to dumbfound anyone momentarily, and the police were no exception. Their sudden shocked indecision was their undoing. Ram Singh's great arms flung wide, seized the police team in a crushing embrace. The breath of each man was expelled in a violent gust; both were unable to cry out, for neither could fill his lungs; two pairs of feet waved and kicked ineffectively, held clear of the floor by Ram Singh's powerful arms, arms that strained ever tighter. A minute or two later and the two bodies slumped unconscious.

"Little men with the blue uniforms," Ram Singh rumbled, a laugh coming from his grinning mouth . "Sleep well! Sleep long!"

As he swung the cops into the hall closet, closing the door, the *Spider* strode into the foyer, Nita cradled in his arms. But Ram Singh held up a warning hand, cocked his head attentively to one side as he listened.

"Sahib," he announced, "others approach. Many others. There is no way but to fight to freedom—and with missie sahib to burden you, how can that be done?"

The *Spider* had heard the dozen police cars draw up in the street below, too. He knew the spot they were in then. Trapped in a murder apartment by a score of cops and at the same time enclosed in a police cordon that circled the whole section! How could the two men hope to break free of that—with an unconscious girl on their hands?

As though to make the crisis even more critical, an ambulance bell stuttered angrily in the street outside; a second called for right-of-way a block or two distant. And it was then an inspirational flash caused the *Spider* to whirl toward Ram Singh.

"There was a butler in here earlier today," he snapped. "Find his white housecoat, Ram Singh! Bring it to me!"

Then the faithful Sikh rushed back into the room with the housecoat a moment later, the *Spider* had disappeared and Richard Wentworth stood in his place, grimly smiling. As he slipped into the coat, Wentworth ordered Ram Singh to rip down the long poles that supported the portiers at either end of the room. Pondering and muttering to himself, the huge servant quickly did as he was told. Had his sahib taken leave of his senses?

The other preparations that followed fast left Ram Singh only more confused. A broom handle was broken in two, lashed across either end of the two longer poles so that an oblong frame, six feet by three, was fashioned. This Richard Wentworth covered with a blanket, tying it securely with twine.

"I am now a doctor—an ambulance intern," Wentworth announced shortly. You are my assistant who helps me carry this stretcher—and the missie sahib is our new patient! The police cannot stop her removal to an ambulance. And to further the deception, Ram Singh, let me have that lipstick you picked up from the floor."

In the space of moments the two men were leaving the apartment, a sheet-covered Nita lying on the improvised stretcher they carried, her face now a mass of hideous red spots.

The first contingent of police met them just at the head of the stairs, but they weren't questioned. Bearing the front end of the improvised stretcher, the white-coated Richard Wentworth easily passed for an ambulance doctor assisting his patient. And in the dimness of the upper hall the incongruous figure of the giant, turbaned Sikh who drew up the rear was not noticed by the hurrying officers.

When the trio started to leave the building, however, it was a different story. Wentworth was passed without immediate question, but a flashlight suddenly sprayed over Ram Singh, illuminating his silk turban, his darkly handsome features and magnificent black beard. The police sergeant on guard at the door, who held the light, gasped in amazement, and Ram Singh showed his shining white teeth in a wide-lipped smile.

"Hey!" the cop exploded. "What goes on here? Who the devil are you, mister?"

It was Wentworth who answered unhesitatingly. "New York Hospital for Contagious Diseases, officer. Emergency call. Stand aside, please—this is urgent."

"No you don't!" the cop snapped. "Stand where you are. Hey, Murphy, Cusak, Benz!"

Three patrolmen pushed up behind the sergeant, awaiting his orders. Open suspicion showed on the face of the jittery sergeant and he flashed his light over Ram Singh again to reassure himself he hadn't been seeing things. Wentworth knew he'd be asked to show his official identification—something he couldn't possibly fake. Without being told, he lowered his end of the stretcher and in doing so let the concealing sheet fall away from Nita's face, seemingly by accident. The tell-tale red splotches—possibly meaning small-pox—showed angrily in the flashlight's beam.

"We can identify ourselves," Wentworth said with assurance. "If you wouldn't mind looking after my patient for a moment, I'll..."

"Wait!" the sergeant yelled, his eyes bulging at sight of the dread splotches. Murphy, Cusak, Benz! Clear a path for the doctor here! Escort him to his ambulance—and fast! You want to keep a poor patient waiting?"

The three patrolmen did as they were told, thrusting through the crowds outside as though the devil himself were behind them. Nor did Richard Wentworth and Ram Singh have to worry about the location of the ambulance; the cops led them directly to it and then speedily disappeared.

Fortunately, the ambulance was empty, except for the driver. The doctor was evidently out on his call, attending to someone who had either been trampled or who had fainted in the crush. The three patrolmen didn't hesitate. They thrust their burden into the vehicle's interior and the driver looked back at them without curiosity until he saw the strangers loading his car. Immediately, then, he challenged them, jumping from his seat and running to the rear of the ambulance.

The following action was so fast it is doubtful if any one of the onlookers understood exactly what happened. Ram Singh seized the man's shoulders, spinning him about, and the heel of one large hand clipped down across the back of the driver's neck. That rabbit punch was beautifully efficient. A second later Ram Singh had disappeared into the interior of the cab with the limp form in his arms, had slammed the doors—and Wentworth had jumped behind the wheel, belling forth a warning clangor as he meshed the gears.

The rest of the journey was fast and easy. Instead of having to fear the surrounding police, the small party was actually aided with all the authority of the city's police force. Blue-coated men jumped to clear intersections as the clanging ambulance approached; traffic obediently pulled to the extreme right to let them pass; even racing patrol cars hugged over to the curb. It is doubtful if the Commissioner of Police himself could have made the trip as fast as they did.

With restoratives he found in a case in the ambulance, Ram Singh managed to revive Nita before the journey was done. When the trio entered Wentworth's apartment building to be whisked up to his penthouse home, Nita walked between Dick and Ram Singh, her face still pale but her strength fast returning.

No sooner had they entered the penthouse, though, then Wentworth saw emergency still existed. In the living room, beside a phonograph, kneeled a nervous, apprehensive Jackson. He held the telephone receiver in his hand—and he was playing a recording into the phone.

Richard Wentworth understood immediately what was happening. Police Commissioner Stanley Kirkpatrick was on the wire! In such an emergency, with Wentworth absent when it was vitally necessary that he be proven to be at home, Jackson had a set of records which would play his master's voice over the wire. These recordings, of course, were of necessity both vague and jocular in their messages. To any question or statement on Kirkpatrick's part, Wentworth would make a flippant and irrelevant reply.

Jackson made violent motions as soon as he saw Wentworth. This sweat-beaded face showed what he had been going through for the past minute or two. Now Wentworth jumped forward and snatched up the receiver as Jackson cut the

Commissioner's angry voice was saying. "I want a clear and sensible reply. It isn't like you to try to hamper the authorities at a time like this! If you persist in your adolescent antics, I'd come around in person and put my questions to you under the authority of..."

"I'm sorry, Kirk," Wentworth broke in, his tone contrite. "I didn't realize things were quite so serious. Furthermore, something just happened

that more or less went to my head—made me sort of dizzy with huffiness. You see, Nita's all right! My alarm for her earlier this evening was entirely unjustified. She's safe and well. There was a simple explanation for the whole misunderstanding. Wouldn't you feel the same way, were it Lona rather than Nita who had turned up safe and sound?"

"I thought you'd gone completely off your rocker," Kirkpatrick answered, somewhat mollified. His next question, though, showed his continued suspicion. "Since we've had the whole Near York

Police force searching for Nita, Dick, would it be too much to ask to hear your so-called simple explanation?

"Of course!" Wentworth said easily. "You know she was out driving the Daimler this evening: keeping some engagement, I think. Anyway, some crook stole the buggy while she had it parked. Then, instead of reporting it missing immediately, she spent some time searching for it. She figured that such an easily spotted car wouldn't be held for long by the hot-car boys. She only returned here an hour ago."

Stanley Kirkpatrick let out a sigh of resignation. "In that case, I suppose, if your Daimler were to be found somewhere on the lower east side, wrecked, Nita wouldn't know a thing about it, just as you wouldn't know anything about a stolen ambulance!"

Richard Wentworth laughed quietly. "Kirk, for a man with an ordinarily enviable mind, you sometimes do think up the silliest questions! Come, come, Commissioner!"

"On top of that," Kirkpatrick snapped back, nettled, "I don't suppose you know anything about the *Spider* being seen near the accident, or of a giant strangely resembling Ram Singh fighting by his side? Or of a case of small-pox..."

"Kirk old man," Richard Wentworth broke in, his tone heavy with sincere concern, "have you been drinking?"

A second later he laughed as the Commissioner's angry growl and the violent breaking of the connection came almost simultaneously.

"The good Commissioner," he told the other three lightly, "is definitely irked. He'll be back at us shortly."

Nita and Ram Singh grinned, knowing the *Spider* had again successfully out-fenced the wily and clever Kirkpatrick. Jackson, though, held his grave expression as he walked over to Wentworth's side. Immediately Wentworth's smile faded.

"Major, there's someone visiting to see you," he announced, his posture and voice that of a sergeant reporting to his superior officer.

"A young girl—and pretty. She's terribly upset, and she says she has to speak to you about her brother—and about the murder-wave that's been terrifying the city. She came about an hour ago and I made her comfortable in the library. Her name is Katherine Whipple Strong and she says you know her family."

Richard Wentworth felt his muscles tense, as though for imminent action. This might be the lead he'd been praying for!

9

TERROR'S CHILDREN

AS HE walked toward the library, Richard Wentworth recalled the Strong family — wealthy, cultured, and part of that fast-vanishing group: the Old New Yorkers. There was Wendell Strong, his wife, Alicia, and two children: James and Katherine. One other relative lived in the city: Jonathan Strong, a brother of Wendell's. The last time Richard Wentworth had dined at the Strong Mansion, however, the two children had been adolescent kids. Now, then he entered the library he realized what two years can mean to a growing girl.

Katherine Strong was a grown woman now, and then she arose to greet him, he was struck by two things—her beauty and her terror. Her makeup had been somewhat marred by the tears she hadn't been able to withhold, and her dark brown eyes that matched her hair, looked at him in dazed, unbelieving fear.

"I'm so glad you'd consent to see me," the girl said in a soft, almost idolizing tone. "In my heart I know you're the only one who can help us now—my brother and me. That's why I came to you, Mr. Wentworth. We're in desperate trouble!"

Richard Wentworth murmured a greeting as he drew up a chair and the very force of his presence, the aura of his assured strength, seemed to comfort the girl immediately. A look of new hope came into her troubled eyes.

"For the sake of an old friendship," Wentworth told her gently, Call me Dick; 'Mr.

Wentworth' makes me feel so ancient! And now tell me what your problem seems to be. I don't believe there's anything we can't manage to straighten out between us."

A faint answering smile told of the girl's new ease. She took a cigarette from the inlaid box at her elbow and lit it before she began to speak in a quiet, even voice. Her first words, though, caused Richard Wentworth's brows to bunch slightly.

"Yesterday, my Uncle Jonathan was murdered. As he sat in his library, he was—was stabbed—and with a hunting knife belonging to my brother! At least, the police claim it belonged to him—and they're searching for him now to place him under arrest!"

"Jonathan Strong murdered," Wentworth repeated in a soft, grim voice. "And it wasn't reported in the papers! That must mean the police are deliberately withholding such news, perhaps fearing its effect on the public. But go on, Katherine."

There isn't a lot I can say, really. In fact, there isn't much that the police know themselves. Uncle Jonathan was murdered in his home; a knife was found, and the police are trying to prove that it belonged to Jimmy; meantime, Jimmy has vanished. I had a talk with him before he left, and we agreed on one thing. Dick, there's a definite pattern behind all these recent, seemingly unrelated murders! And out of that pattern one terrible, frightening fact was clear to us!"

Richard Wentworth looked at the girl more closely; he had thought he was the only one to have definitely spotted one fact behind the crime wave. The Strong kids had certainly been doing some straight thinking. He waited for her to continue.

"All of these murders seem to have no connection, no possible relationship pointing to one group of criminals. Yet I've noticed that whenever the police dig up a possible suspect, a possible witness to the crime, that suspect or witness is mysteriously and promptly slain— before the police can go one step further."

"In our case, Jimmy was suspected of Uncle Jonathan's death. That meant he was directly on the spot. We agreed that even if it did tend to involve him further, the only way to save his life was to hide out from both the police—and the criminals who would instantly cut him down in cold blood."

Wentworth nodded a silent agreement. "Do you know where your brother is presently hiding?" he asked.

Now the girl nodded. "There's a little story behind it," she explained. "About a year ago Jim fell in love with a nice young girl. As the romance went on, they even spoke of marriage. At that point, the family stepped in—headed by Uncle Jonathan. You see, the girl didn't come from a wealthy or prominent family; she was alone in the world and worked in a run-of-the-mill department store. As a result, Jim pretended to fall in with their wishes but he continued to see her secretly. That deception was necessary since Jim figured prominently in Uncle Jonathan's will and he would otherwise have been cut off without a penny."

Wentworth whistled softly. "Then your brother profited handsomely by Jonathan Strong's death! No wonder the police are sure he wielded the murder weapon! So, Katherine, I suppose the two of you decided to hide Jim out at the girl's apartment?"

"Mary Hicks took him in without hesitation, even though it could mean a jail sentence or death!" she said.

Wentworth arose, concluding the conference. "We're going to pay Mary Hicks a visit—and immediately. It's possible your brother can give us another fact or two before our next campaign begins. Let's go, Katherine."

When Richard Wentworth and Katherine Strong entered the living room, Nita turned quickly from the radio. She had been listening to the news reports, and one item reminded her of an experience she had had earlier that night. Briefly, she told Dick about her meeting with Silas Breen, the wealthy reformer and proselytizing evangelist, and of his determination to tackle the crime-wave alone, in Wentworth's absence.

"He tried it, too, in his blind innocence," she concluded. "There was just a flash on the air that he had been found unconscious in the street, badly beaten. It's lucky for him that the underworld didn't know he possessed inside information; they'd have exterminated him as quickly as the others. I tried to stop him, Dick, but he wouldn't listen!"

"If things go right," Wentworth told her with quiet determination, "Breen will be avenged—and so will a hundred others who've suffered far more than he. Wait here for me, Nita; I'll be back in an hour or two and after that there will be plenty of work for all of us. Dangerous work, I'm afraid."

"Dick!" Nita broke out. Where are you going now? Why don't you take Jackson or Ram Singh with you?"

There was troubled apprehension in her tone and Richard Wentworth smiled at her gently. He went up to her and took her in his arms for a moment, holding her close. His lips brushed hers, and then he had suddenly released her and was striding quickly toward the foyer hall—here Katherine waited for him. Jackson, Ram Singh and Nita watched his broad-shouldered, retreating back, the same agonizing thought in the minds of all of them, as always. Would Richard Wentworth come back?

A cab whisked Wentworth and the girl uptown and into the Bronx. When they finally arrived at the address, dawn was already beginning to brush the eastern sky with the bright promise of a new day. Both of them realized that for them, as for the millions of other people in the great metropolis, this could also be an eventful day, the outcome of which could affect the lives of all who lived in the city of New York.

The house Mary Hicks lived in was typical of the section; it was a respectable but a cheap walk-up, indistinguishable from a hundred others that huddled shoulder-to-shoulder in the surrounding blocks. It made an excellent hide-out.

Mary lived on the top floor of the five-story building, and after Wentworth had pushed the bell his quick ears caught the sound of stealthy footsteps within. No one answered the door, however; there was no response to his second and third rings, either. It was only after Katherine, her brown eyes big with fright again, had knocked sharply with her knuckles and called Jim's name softly that movement was again heard inside. The door opened several inches, further opening prevented by a stout chain, and a girl's white face peered out at them.

Mary recognized Katherine at once, and a moment later she had released the chain and they were inside. The shades of the two-room apartment were tightly drawn, a floor lamp in the living room giving the only illumination. Standing there in the middle of the floor, his body half crouched and tense, Wentworth saw Jimmy Strong. He seemed to be half out of his mind with fear.

''Richard Wentworth!" the pretty blonde greeted him. "I didn't know... You see, everyone who approaches—even strangers—are possible enemies and killers."

James Strong had come forward to greet them now, his fear dissolving as he recognized his callers. "Kay! And Wentworth!" he said with relief. "For the first time I'm beginning to feel that maybe there is some hope, after all."

"There's more than hope," Wentworth said with assurance. All we need is information— enough for a starting point. That's where you come in, Strong—and there's not a moment to lose!"

10

The Growing Peril

A moment later the little group was seated in the small, tidy living room. And Richard Wentworth's request of Strong had been simple: to tell all he knew about the crime. His response was disappointing, however. He could tell no more than Katherine had already revealed.

"There was one strange experience I had, though," he concluded. "I didn't mention it to Kay before because I thought it could only make things look blacker to her. It was something I did, and it seems to strengthen the case against me."

"And that was?" Wentworth prompted the reluctant youth.

"It happened about ten days ago," James Strong explained. "I was at a dinner party with several friends of the family. After eating, we sat around and had a couple of brandies—but only a couple. That's the funny part of it. All of a sudden, the drink seemed to hit me; I felt as though I'd had ten glasses, I was so woozy. I don't remember why I got angry, or what I said—but friends told me afterward."

"You threatened the life of your uncle?" Wentworth suggested.

Jim Strong looked startled. "Why, yes," he replied. "So I'm told. I'll admit I was particularly sore at Uncle Jonathan that day. I'd been brooding about Mary, and how we probably could have been married by then if Uncle Jonathan hadn't influenced my family, made them forbid the ceremony. And it seems I shouted out that I wished he were dead, that I'd like to see him dead, to kill him myself. More remarks of the same sort followed, until the others got me out of the place. Of course I don't know what made me say such things, or who overheard me at the surrounding tables. But, Mr. Wentworth, I swear I wouldn't have made any such remarks If I'd been in my right mind. I swear to you I don't really feel that way. I swear on my word I didn't kill Jonathan Strong!"

"I know you didn't," he answered with conviction, his eyes taking in the clean-cut youth's features. "The fact still remains, though, that he's dead, murdered; that all the evidence points to you; and that you're definitely on the spot, both by the police and by the underworld."

"It's hopeless," young Strong said. "I'm going to do now what I threatened before. I'm going to clear out of Mary's apartment. I won't have anything happen to her because of me!"

"Hold it, boy, Richard Wentworth said quietly. "First of all, tell me exactly who was with you on this dinner party."

"Oh, you couldn't suspect anyone there of any trickery," Jim told him. "They were all close friends of the family. There was Dr. Lytell— Harrison Lytell—who's been our personal physician for years. There where two college friends of mine—both of whom left the city the next day and who haven't been back since. And there was a friend of Dad's and Uncle Jonathan's: Silas Breen."

"Silas Breen?" Wentworth repeated, wondering. "Could it be possible he saw some lead to the thugs behind these crimes through the events of that evening? He discovered something somewhere and suffered a beating for his pains."

"It's possible," Jim Strong agreed. "But there's only one man who can answer that. Silas Breen."

"Exactly," Wentworth said. "So he's the one I'm going to ask.

Meantime, I'm going to find another hide-out for you for Mary's protection. That way, there will only be the two of us who will know your whereabouts and no possible slip can be made."

Richard Wentworth knew, though he didn't say it aloud, that anyone—who was aware of Jim Strong's whereabouts would be as much on the death spot as the boy himself.

It was early morning when Wentworth and Strong left the apartment with Mary and Katherine. The two girls, Wentworth put into a cab, Mary to go to her job and Katherine to continue on home. Then because that section of the Bronx was well suited to a hide-out, and because there was little time to lose, he searched about until he found a room for Jim in a family's apartment. That way, he could reach the boy by phone, should necessity arise.

During the drive to Breen's home, Richard Wentworth realized with growing despair the shortness of time left to him and the lack of progress he seemed to be making. He knew well the *Spider*'s cardinal rule of underworld warfare always attack, especially when things look the worst! When disaster threatens—attack, attack! And he decided that this interview with Silas Breen would be his last attempt for knowledge through investigation. Immediately thereafter, no matter what the outcome, the underworld would feel the might of the *Spider* in whatever quarter presented itself. There was no more precious time to be lost!

Silas Breen was something of a mystery-man in New York City. There were those who said he had once been a great industrialist, owner of vast corporations, who had pyramided his holding companies until the inevitable crash had come. Then, suddenly "getting religion" he had changed his name and come east, still with enough money to be called a rich man.

New York, too, had difficulty in understanding him since his arrival. Was he a fake, fanatic or a puritan philanthropist? Did he mean what he preached from the hired platforms of the city's vast tabernacles? Or was there some scheming method of profit in his repeated supplications for people to repent and reform? The most popular belief was that Silas Breen had a sincere message to bring before the world—but that his fervor to have it told and heeded had driven him somewhat beyond the mentally normal.

Upon his arrival in the city some years before he had bought a private home on the west side in the lower eighties. The mansion had at one time been the pride of the neighborhood, but age and neglect had reduced it to a pathetic monument to decay and slow ruin. Nevertheless, the huge house still stood, well within its on grounds. Even the taxes on the place cost a fortune each year and no one but the eccentric Silas Breen would have bothered maintaining such a costly wreck.

Breen kept no servants. He lived alone, but was constantly admitting a stream of callers to his home. Most of them were the shabby, down-at heels men—reformed criminals—whom he sought to "save" and rehabilitate for society. Needless to say, the other wealthy homes of the section would gladly have paid Breen to move away, had he been the type to accept such a proposition.

Richard Wentworth strode up the broken-flagged walk that wound through the weed-grown lawn. The bell beside the shabby, paint-flaking front door wouldn't work, so he rapped on the panel. Almost immediately the door was opened by Breen, as though he had been observing Wentworth's approach through one of the dirt begrimed windows. A smile of welcome lighted his face.

''Wentworth!'' he exclaimed. "How I've been hoping to get in touch with you. Called your home a number of times, you know; no satisfaction. But you're here, anyway. Come in, come in!"

Wentworth was observing the cuts and lumps on Breen's face evidence of the beating he'd received. One eye was nearly closed and his left hand was bandaged. As he ushered Wentworth through the large two-story reception hall, he walked with a decided limp.

Whatever else he might have been, the man was certainly no coward. Wentworth pondered if he realized how lucky he was to have escaped with his life— or if he knew how quickly he would have been killed had the underworld suspected he had any inside knowledge.

The musty, oppressive odor of the dank atmosphere was heavy in Wentworth's nostrils as they crossed an enormous, sparsely furnished living room. But the smaller library beyond was really quite livable. Here some effort had been made at comfort and cleanliness, and the satisfying smell of cigar smoke filled the room.

Silas Breen sank into a chair behind a heavy, carved desk and motioned Richard Wentworth to an easy chair at one side.

"You have come to me, Mr. Wentworth," Breen began, "so that must mean you have something to tell me. You can trust me with any confidence, as you know, but it isn't difficult to guess your purpose here. Not with this wave of evil steeping the city."

Wentworth took a cigarette from his case, tapped it lightly. "You're wrong on one point," he remarked quietly. "I didn't come here to tell you anything; I came here to ask you a question. To be specific: Just that was it you wanted to tell me last evening? What information did you have— and who told it to you?"

The change that came over Silas Breen was startling. His entire expression changed in a flash and his eyes darted nervously about the room, as though looking for eavesdroppers. The man was plainly frightened. He held up his hand as though to caution Wentworth against saying anything more.

"Please!" he begged. "Let's not go into that. As a matter of fact, I have investigated what suspicions I may have had and I have found them groundless. Whatever I may have said to Miss van Sloan was spoken too quickly. I deeply regret the indiscretion of my words."

Richard Wentworth looked long at his host, holding the other's eyes until Breen's gaze fell. Had Silas Breen really learned something and then been terrified into silence and a flat denial?

Such a conclusion didn't fit in with the other known side of Breen's character. He was no coward; it would take something far from the ordinary to frighten him this way. Had he been threatened by some fantastic power of evil—some power that threatened far more than his life? Or was he an out-and-out charlatan—worse, a clever criminal in a philanthropist's disguise? None of those explanations satisfied Wentworth then.

"Mr. Breen," Richard Wentworth said evenly, "you did learn something behind the crimes that flood the city with innocent blood! When you deny it, you are a liar!"

II

THE UNDERWORLD STRIKES!

SILAS BREEN'S hands had come up to grip the edge of the
desk until the knuckles grew white, the fingers trembled. His
breathing was labored and heavy. For a long moment he didn't
speak, evidently not trusting his voice. It was obvious he wasn't
used to being spoken to in such a way. At last, though, a certain
control seemed to return to him, though his face remained pale.

"Look at it this way, Breen," Wentworth pressed on. "For some
time you've devoted your energy, time and money to the uprooting
of evil in this city. Then, only yesterday, you apparently learned
something concerning the greatest evil tide that has ever swept over
this metropolis. You told Nita van Sloan you had learned something
of vital importance, and that it was urgent you see me immediately.
When that was impossible, you risked your very life to investigate
the knowledge yourself.

"Now, though, you refuse to tell me that you knew—-or
suspected. You seem terrified. Is that being fair to the very people
on whom you have lavished your efforts for reform?—could any of
them seriously listen to you again if they knew of this act?

"Yet my request is simple. Just tell me what you suspected.
After that, the matter of action is in my hands alone—and I won't

disappoint you in what I do. It will be done well."

Richard Wentworth was silent for a moment, then demanded with a force that couldn't be denied, "Silas Breen, what did you learn about the East Side Bar that made you go there alone?"

Breen took a deep breath before he replied. It was obviously costing him a great effort. "One of my converts came to me," he said at last in a voice so low it could scarcely be heard. "He reported that the organization behind these multiple murders—and it is an organization— could call a meeting of its officers for last evening. The meeting place, of course, was the East Side Bar. For that reason, I went there—foolishly.

"No one of any consequence showed up while I was there. I had probably been spotted; my presence had scared them away. And all I gained was a sound thrashing at the hands of a gang of bullies."

"What was his name?" Wentworth demanded.

"Peruez," Breen said after a slight hesitation. "Ralphael Peruez."

Richard Wentworth racked his memory for details of the gangster named Peruez. All he remembered that was pertinent was that Peruez was a small-time hoodlum whose gun was for hire to the highest bidder. Beyond that—and the fact that Peruez, known to the underworld as "The Rat", was also a pint-sized knife-wielding punk— he could recall little. It was Peruez associates who could be his only lead now.

"Where can I find him?" he asked. "When did you hear from him last?"

Breen got that scared look on his face again. ''That's just it, Wentworth. I have not seen or heard from him since yesterday, when he gave me that information. Since he was supposed to have gotten in touch with me long ago, I haven't the slightest doubt but that he's dead—murdered for having talked!"

"Very well, then," Wentworth persisted, "tell me—"

He broke off then,—whirling as his hand jumped for his gun. That noise at the window! Even as Silas Breen screamed, Wentworth saw the small figure framed in the window! saw his arm flash forward to send a knife streaking through the air toward the reformer! Wentworth's gun thundered, the window shattered with the sound— but the target had dropped from view but a split-second before.

Behind him, Richard Wentworth could hear Silas Breen still screaming in a high, terrified voice, like that of a woman's. He knew the other wasn't badly wounded; knew he was still on his feet. Without a seconds hesitation, Wentworth raced out of the library, through the living room and foyer, skidding to a stop on the front porch. Ahead, he saw the sprinting figure of the little gunman and knife thrower almost to the high front gate.

Wentworth's snap-shot was unerring. In a flailing heap the thug went down, a bullet in his calf which was exactly as Wentworth wanted it. There was much valuable information the assailant could give—and would give! He had to be taken alive.

Running forward more easily now, Wentworth approached his squealing captive— and suddenly hurled himself face down upon the ground with the speed and ease he had gained in the shell-blasted battlefields of France! The chattering tommy-gun chopped out its song of death for a full ten seconds before it ceased. And by that time Wentworth knew he hadn't been its intended target—and knew, as certainly, that he no longer had a captive who could talk.

One glance at the still body was enough as he raced past. And then, then the urgent roar of a powerful motorcar sounded up the street, Wentworth knew that further chase was hopeless. But it was only after the emergency of the battle was over that Richard Wentworth felt the searing burn cutting along his left side and knew that he had been hit during the fray. A ricocheting bullet, perhaps— or, more probably, a deliberate pot-shot by one of the others in the party of assassins had managed to nick him.

Still hoping the riddled knife-thrower could give him some information, even though dead, he walked back to the huddled, blood spattered form. An inside pocket held a ragged wallet—and in the transparent compartment Wentworth saw a driver's license. The name on it made him wrinkle his brow in wonder. Ralphael Peruez, the name read, and a signet ring on the hand of the corpse verified that name with its initials.

Richard Wentworth knew it would be useless to return to Breen's home in the hope of more information. If the philanthropist had been frightened before, he was undoubtedly hysterical now. He probably wouldn't even admit his own name. Furthermore, it was time for the *Spider* to attack! There could be no more delay.

Driving back to his apartment in a taxi, Wentworth puzzled for a moment over the strange case of a gunman giving out information freely, and then trying to murder the person he'd talked to simply because he was repeating that information. To that, there mere two possible answers: first, that the information given to Breen had had but one purpose: to lure the philanthropist to an underworld trap. That possibility was out, since Silas Breen had seen nothing, heard nothing, and had been allowed to return alive. The second possibility was that the small-time gunman had really learned something, which he had repeated and then had been ordered by the gang, on pain of death for himself, to kill the person he'd talked to. That was it, then. Instead of liquidating Peruez for his loose tongue, the gang had assigned him the task of undoing the damage he'd caused.

Why had Peruez been exterminated, if that was so? Because he had failed? No—because the waiting gang members couldn't have known that. He had been killed because he was on the point of capture—just as everyone else who could possibly give the Police a lead to the source of the murders were exterminated, innocent or not! No one, not even a member of' the gang would be allowed to fall into the hands of the police!

And, as he realized that, Richard Wentworth suddenly knew what he had to do—and a shudder passed through his athletic body. The plan that had just come to him—a desperate, wild plan was his only possible hope of breaking the ring of secrecy that ruthless murder had erected about this underworld plague!

If the gang immediately set out after any person suspected of having knowledge of the underworld empire, however slight that knowledge might be—then Richard Wentworth would adopt the identity of one such person and set himself up as a clay pigeon for the guns of that gang! His one hope—if it could be called a hope—was that he'd be taken to the criminals headquarters for extermination, and that he could, single handed, smash that crime empire before his death sentence was completed!

Wentworth's face was bitterly set as the cab drew up before his fashionable residence. He had already decided on the identity he'd assume—that of young Jimmy Strong, so eagerly sought by the underworld! And if the underworld—was looking for him so urgently, he knew, too, just where he'd go to reveal himself.

He'd go to the East Side Bar, focal point of so much of the gang's activity!

12

GALLANT CHALLENGE

NITA VAN SLOAN, Ram Singh and Jackson all smiled happily with relief as Richard Wentworth walked debonairly into the spacious apartment. He was back again—but they didn't yet know his present plan, one that had to be undertaken immediately. It was Nita who spoke first, her voice banteringly gay.

"Not so much as a telephone call, Dick, my dear," she told him. "You've been ignored—even by your staunch friend and personal nemesis, the Police Commissioner. You're slipping, darling."

Wentworth put on an expression of mock sadness and Ram Singh rumbled in his beard. It was Jackson, closer to Wentworth than the others, who noticed the look of drawn paleness on his master's face. He grasped him by the arm.

"Major!" he exclaimed, his voice concerned. "You don't look so hot. Nothing's happened? You're..."

"Weary," Wentworth told him, smiling faintly. "Just a bit weary, Jackson. It'll pass."

He didn't want to alarm Nita by mentioning the wound he'd received. By now his whole side was pulsing with an intermittent, throbbing fire; it hurt him to use his left arm, and he had to force himself to walk without a limp. He knew he had lost a lot of blood; the lightness in his head told him that.

After a moment or two, on a pretext, he got Ram Singh to leave the room with him. Back in the bedroom, he stripped to the waist and nodded to the first-aid kit on the chiffonier.

"Need a bit of patching up, Ram Singh," he said. "Can do?"

The expression on the giant Singh's face was one of alarm but he would never admit as much to his sahib.

"A scratch," he dismissed the wound scornfully. "Such a mere tickle of lead as I would never even feel—though, I'll admit, it might cause little Jackson to faint. Wah! Anyway, as a display of my skill, I'll bind it, sahib!"

Even as he spoke, his hands had been busy with the antiseptic, and now he neatly applied— bandage and adhesive, not only dressing the wound but taping up Wentworth's left side as well. As he did so, Wentworth outlined his plan to throw himself deliberately into the hands of the underworld by assuming the identity of young Jim Strong. Ram Singh's breath made a sound in his nostrils and there was a rumble in his throat—a sure sign he didn't approve.

"Sahib," he said with that impressive dignity he could sometimes assume, "a coward fears death; a brave man dares it with a challenge. But only a fool deliberately welcomes it!"

Dressed again, Richard Wentworth ignored the Sikh's wise council, pretending not to have heard.

"Bring the make-up kit into the living room, Ram Singh."

"Sahib, there is great misfortune," Ram Singh told him, his voice heavy with desolation. "The box of a thousand faces is nowhere to be found! It is gone, lost!"

"It's on the dresser, in plain sight," Wentworth said quietly, a faint smile on his lips, and then left the room.

In the living room a strained silence held Nita and Jackson as he repeated his desperate plan. When he had finished, it was Nita van Sloan who spoke first.

"Dick, you must be mad!" she exclaimed. "I won't let you do it!

You must be mad!"

"I am mad, Nita, darling," he replied with a smile. "That, perhaps, is my greatest charm—if any. I'm slightly mad—and you will let me do it."

"Dick, you listen to me?" the lovely girl persisted, her voice heavy with the urgency of her

fear for him. "There's a world of difference between being brave—and being foolhardy! This thing you suggest can help no one. You intend to walk into a trap of your own making, disguised as Jim Strong and, after being seized and slated for execution, you hope to smash single handedly a crime empire that has defied the whole New York City police force! Dick, even a child could see that it won't work!"

"Ram Singh, open the box of a thousand faces," Wentworth ordered, his voice adamant. "Help me prepare."

Reluctantly, the giant Sikh did as he was told. Studiously, however, he kept his eyes averted from those of his missie sahib. He had experienced before this clash of wills—and he knew her eyes would implore him to knock his sahib unconscious rather than allow him to go to his certain death. Under such pressure, his affection for both was on the rack.

Minutes passed as Richard Wentworth's skillful fingers went busily about the change of personality. At his elbow, Ram Singh stood ready with bleach, dye, gum Arabic, tweezers, and skin putty. Finally, as though a miracle had taken place before their very eyes, those in the room looked upon Richard Wentworth no longer. The debonair clubman and insouciant man-about-town had ceased to exist. In his place stood James Strong, a clean-cut young man in his early twenties, newly graduated from college and not yet quite sure of himself in the austere circles of fashionable society. It was truly a miracle.

"Nothing I can say will influence you, I suppose," Nita said now, her eyes averted and her voice low.

"Nita, darling!" Wentworth exclaimed. ''To listen to you, one would think this was the first time I'd ever set out alone on an adventure that wasn't entirely safe."

"The first time?" Nita repeated. "No, Dick, I wasn't thinking that. I was thinking it is probably the last!"

But when she looked up again, he was standing in the foyer wearing a snap-brim hat and a raglan topcoat—an outfit such as Jim habitually wore. Underneath, of course, he wore his gun— and carried those other aids necessary to Wentworth and the *Spider*. All the same, the challenge he was flinging down to the underworld seemed terribly one-sided.

"Wait for me here," he called to them gaily. "When I return it will be with victory. There'll be champagne for all hands!"

But none of them smiled as he left the apartment.

When Richard Wentworth assumed the physical appearance of another, it was with an uncanny genius for detail he also assumed the exact personality, the minute mannerisms, of the character he impersonated. Indeed, he had trained himself even to think like that person. That gift had stood him in good stead on many an occasion.

Dusk was fast falling on the city, and in the narrow streets of the east-side slums a sort of false night had already arrived. The East Side Bar had its usual score of customers in attendance and they looked up with surprise as the boyish stranger pushed through the doors. He stood somewhat hesitantly just inside, his eyes searching the room as though looking for someone. After a moment the young man walked over to the bar, his gait a studied and somewhat clumsy copy of self assurance. It was exactly as Jim Strong would have behaved in this atmosphere.

"Well, sonny?" the beefy bartender asked. The tone of his voice and his surly attitude plainly said that the newcomer wasn't wanted and that it could be healthier for him elsewhere.

Jim Strong ignored the hint. "Give me a beer," he said.

"You sure it won't go to your head, Sonny?" the beefy man said.

Strong ignored the second remark too. His eyes were examining the characters in the room, a dangerous pastime for any stranger in such a place as this.

"You looking for somebody, maybe?" The threat in the bartenders voice was now raw and naked, like a knife drawn.

"As a matter of fact, I am," Jim Strong replied. "I left a message for Silas Breen to meet me here. He must be late."

"Any name you mention," the bartender pointed out with ominous quiet, "I never heard of the guy. Understand? But if there is such a guy as this Breen, and he's ever been here before, I don't think he'll be back. In fact, I'm sure of it!"

Jim Strong didn't say why he'd asked Silas Breen to meet him here, or how he'd ever heard of the bar in the first place. He let that hang in the air for the bartender to worry about. And he realized, too, that a dozen pair of ears were taking in his every word. The mention of Breen's name had brought a dead hush over the room. An electric tension quivered in the atmosphere.

"Maybe you don't know who I am?" Jim Strong said, a petulant note in his voice. "I'm Jim Strong and Breen's been a friend of my Uncle Jonathan Strong for years. He'll keep the date."

The bartender said, "I see," and he said it very quietly, his words almost a whisper.

Strong knew this trap of his own making was complete now. He watched the bartender drum out a signal on the bar with the stubby fingers of his right hand—and saw, from the corner of his eye, one of the customers get to his feet and walk casually over to the telephone booth in the corner. There could be no turning back now if, for the first time in his life, Richard Wentworth, or any of his characters, had ever turned back.

For perhaps five minutes longer Jim Strong lounged at the bar, the untasted glass of beer standing in front of him. He could almost feel the eyes that steadily watched his back for his every move, and a sense of approaching danger ran through him. His choice had been made—and his life hung in the balance.

After another period of waiting, Strong suddenly pushed the glass of beer away from him irritably. "The hell with it," he exploded angrily. "If Breen doesn't want to hear what I had to tell him, others do. The newspapers, for instance."

"Why, sure," the beefy bartender agreed, his face breaking into a wolfish grin that showed his broken and blackened teeth. "That's one thing a man can always do—talk. It's his right. As long as he lives, he can talk. As long as he lives!"

But Jim Strong pretended not to have heard him. He turned from the bar without undue haste and started for the door. Behind him he heard chairs scrape and knew that three, perhaps four, men had risen to follow him. Obviously, they wouldn't want trouble right in the bar; they'd wait until he got to the street outside, here reinforcements probably waited.

When he reached the sidewalk, Strong turned to the left and started to walk slowly away. The men who had followed him crossed the street and began to parallel his course. After a moment,

he increased his pace and was surprised when the trailers didn't match him. Instead, they let him increase the distance between them as much as he desired. Then, suddenly, he saw why a half a block ahead, a second pair of men strolled. It was obvious, then, that no matter how fast or slow he went—and on any neighboring street a pair of thugs would have him under observation. The trap had been neatly closed.

Abruptly, disaster swept upon the scene! Coming down the street Jim Strong saw a big Daimler idling along—a second car of his that he rarely used—and the great-bearded, fierce-fighting Ram Singh sat at the wheel, his huge frame making even that big car look small! And beside him sat Nita van Sloan! They had followed him into the trap!

The one reason Wentworth had walked into the underworld alone, in Jim Strong's personality, was because of the chances against him. He wouldn't have thought of taking Ram Singh along—and far less would he had considered taking Nita! Yet, here they were, unasked, coming to his side!

Instantly he saw the car, Jim Strong ceased walking, turned into a doorway as though to light a cigarette and presented his back to the street. He actually held his breath as the softly purring motor approached—then expelled it in relief as it continued past. If they only hadn't seen him!

Then, deciding to get the business over with once and for all, he suddenly whirled out of the doorway and began to sprint down the dark street. A shout went up behind him, followed by a warning whistle. An answering whistle sounded ahead and, surprising him with their efficiency, men closed in on him from all sides, their pounding feet echoing ahead, behind, to right and left!

A hurtling weight struck Strong from the back, down at the knees, and brawny arms wrapped about his racing legs. One second he had been running—the next he had hit the pavement with jarring force, was rolling and skidding along the sidewalk. His tackler had had the advantage, bracing himself beforehand and planning the fall so that Strong landed on the bottom. Also, Strong's wounded side gave him excruciating agony in that violent encounter. Dizziness swept over him; he had to fight to retain his reeling senses. But it didn't do any good. Before he could so much as lift his arms, a stunning blow caught him on the temple; another crashed down on the back of his skull. The street spun crazily—and a blackness deeper than the night swept over him.

With his last conscious thought he wondered if they'd kill him where he lay, defenseless and helpless....

13

IS THERE STILL TIME?

AFTER Richard Wentworth had left, disguised as Jim Strong, Nita, Jackson and Ram Singh sat about the apartment in gloomy silence for long minutes. Occasionally Ram Singh would make a deep growling noise in his great chest, then rise to his feet and stalk the length of the room before being reseated. Nita neither moved or spoke. Jackson sat at a table, busily engaged in cleaning and oiling the Army-issue Colt .45 he'd carried in the last war. It was his only substitute for action. Finally Ram Singh, the battle loving giant, could stand it no longer.

"I like this not!" he rumbled. "There is a feeling within me. It is not well that we sit here idly like old women at a fireside!"

"What would you do, Ram Singh?" Nita van Sloan asked, her voice almost pleading for some suggestion.

"Follow him, missie sahib!" the huge, turbaned Sikh urged. "We could not stop the sahib; that he would not hear of. We could not accompany him; he insisted on a solitary journey. But he said nothing about following him. Thus, should a sudden, unexpected danger loom, we would be close at hand. Wah! With his knife, Ram Singh would rip and slash that danger! He would make of it a piteous and begging thing!"

Jackson made a depreciating sound from across the room and Ram Singh turned to glower at him. Nita, though, was looking at the fierce black-bearded man with new hope in her eyes.

"Follow Dick," she mused. Then, coming to an abrupt decision, she was on her feet. "Ram Singh, we'll do it!'

"By the sacred beard of Kali!," he exulted. "Action! Wah!"

Jackson, too, had come to his feet, the eager light of coming battle in his eyes. For a moment Nita's face was troubled.

"We can't all go," she pointed out. "'Someone has to stay here and stand guard by the telephone." Her eyes went to Jackson. "Ram Singh doesn't understand mechanical devices, Jackson and, should the Commissioner telephone, one of those recordings would be vital to the Major's alibi. So I'm afraid..."

"I know," Jackson broke in, his voice dejected. "Don't rub it in, Miss van Sloan. I'm elected again."

"Play your music box, little man!" Ram Singh exulted. "Make sounds and words come from the magic wood, like an old man amusing himself harmlessly while the fighters are away. Ram Singh, the great warrior, goes to the battle!"

Nita spoke quickly now, interrupting the clash. She knew of the jealous rivalry between these two men, each wanting to serve his master best. And, for the moment, she felt sorry for Jackson.

"The sahib told you where he would go, Ram Singh?" she asked.

The Sikh nodded importantly. "In the bedroom, as I was dressing his wound. He goes to that small bar he visited before."

Ram Singh, who looked upon a wound as an honorable and distinguished decoration earned in battle, thought nothing of mentioning such a fact to Nita. He didn't even notice her quick gasp and the way her hand came up quickly to cover her mouth. Nita recovered herself quickly, though, losing her new fear in the promise of the coming action.

"Let's go quickly to the garage," she said.

"There isn't any time to lose."

But five minutes later, driving quickly downtown, she had time to think again of Dick's desperate gamble and of the odds against him. And to try such a thing while wounded! But Ram Singh, behind the wheel, was complacent. He hummed a happy fighting song from his native land, impatient for the fray.

Once in the slum district, Nita began her sharp vigil as they drove along, her eyes searching for any sight of Dick. Ram Singh watched his side of the street, driving automatically with only an occasional glance ahead. As they approached the hide-out bar, Nita became aware of the strange number of loiterers they passed and she knew they were already within the trap. Her heart was pounding fast now. She knew the danger Dick was in; though he had

tried to make light of the whole thing, she had seen the strangely troubled, almost apprehensive, look in his eyes.

Once, when they were about three blocks from their destination, Nita thought she saw Dick ahead. Not that she could distinguish features in that gloomy canyon through which they drove, but the light of a street lamp momentarily silhouetted a man of about Dick's build. One of Nita's small hands went quickly to Ram Singh's arm in warning—and then fell away. The figure she had been watching had suddenly turned from the sidewalk and entered one of the rotting tenement houses. She had been mistaken; it was simply a trick of the night and her own anxiety.

Then, in front of the East Side Bar at last, both she and Ram Singh knew bitter defeat, complete frustration. The place was dark, with simply a dim bulb burning in the rear. It had obviously closed up for the night.

So great was their feeling of empty helplessness that neither gave conscious heed to a sudden whistle from down the street—nor to the answering whistle, further off, that floated back. They couldn't have heard at that distance, of course, the sudden pounding of feet that had followed the two whistles.

"Something has gone wrong, missie sahib," Ram Singh said sadly.

"Everything has gone wrong," Nita told him quietly. "And there's no where else for us to turn. We'd best go back to the apartment and hope against hope."

Somehow, as though in a nightmare, Wentworth as Jim Strong remembered a long ride in an automobile. The meaning of the ride, of who or where he was, didn't penetrate his consciousness. And if it hadn't been for the sensation of pain in his head and side, it's probable he wouldn't even have been dimly aware of the jolting movement that only increased his torment. After a time, though, blackness returned—and with it all sensation ceased.

Back in Richard Wentworth's apartment, Ronald Jackson paced the floor impatiently for a time. During this particular adventure he felt as though he'd been left out of things, neglected. It had been Ram Singh who had gone to the Major's aid the night before, while he waited quietly at this post for possible developments. And this evening it had been Ram Singh again, with Nita van Sloan, who had sallied forth to give battle in the master's support. To Jackson, this was all wrong. Ronald Jackson was a man of action too; he was a fighter and he wanted a fight.

After a time, though, he mastered his impatience. He sat in an easy chair quietly, but he glowered at the silent telephone, hoping it could ring to tell him of impending action. It didn't ring. Strangely, it was the doorbell that chimed its soft notes to tell of a visitor.

Scowling in puzzlement, Jackson walked into the foyer hall, but he didn't answer the summons immediately. Could this be some sort of trap for the Major? Opening a small compartment beside the door, he looked into a concealed mirror device that revealed the person calling without that caller being aware of the scrutiny.

Outside, twisting her gloves nervously, stood a young girl. It was young Mary Hicks, Jim Strong's pretty little sweetheart— though Jackson did not recognize her. He knew, though, that she was in trouble.

As soon as Jackson opened the door, Mary entered quickly. Her greeting to him was perfunctory, telling of an urgent alarm she felt. Her quick-searching eyes covered the living room, came back to Jackson anxiously.

"Is Mr. Wentworth here?" she asked, almost pleadingly. "It's desperately important that I see him!"

Jackson shook his head slowly. "Sorry, Miss," he told her. "I don't expect him back for some time yet. But is there anything I could do to help?"

The haunting fear in Mary's eyes increased with the news. "It's about Jim," she explained quickly. "I'm Mary Hicks and Jim Strong is my fiancee. And it's a matter of life and death! Are you sure there isn't anyway I could reach Richard Wentworth?"

Again Jackson shook his head, regretfully.

"Then you'll help me, won't you? Please!" Her voice broke slightly with the urgency of her appeal; one small hand went out to rest supplicatingly on Jackson's arm. "They've got Jim! Those killers have made him prisoner! And I'm afraid to go to the police. They'd only arrest me for concealing a fugitive—and indict him for the murder of his uncle! Don't you see how—"

"Are you sure of that?" Jackson broke in. "Are you sure the boy's been actually seized?"

"I saw it!" Mary replied. "Mr. Wentworth took Jim from my apartment, found him other quarters. But he couldn't stand being away from me when I was in danger. He telephoned me to ask if I was all right. Then he said he had to go outside for some cigarettes and asked me to meet him at the corner for a moment. I agreed. Outside, I saw him standing at the end of the block—but before

I could get to him, a car swung up to the curb and a gang of men jumped out. They didn't give Jim a chance—and a moment later they were back in the car, dragging him with them!"

Jackson whistled softly. "That's proof enough!" he said. "And you haven't any idea who these men were—or where they've taken Jim Strong?"

Mary's answer was surprising. "I know where he's been taken, because I followed the kidnap car in a taxi. That's why I rushed directly to Mr. Wentworth for help! Someone has got to make them set Jim free! You will do it, won't you?"

Ronald Jackson didn't answer right away. He had been given strict orders by Nita van Sloan to stand by in the apartment and Jackson had never disobeyed orders before. But another factor had entered the situation now, a factor that was always uppermost in the ex-sergeant's mind: the Major's safety. For if what the girl told him was true—and he knew it was—then it wouldn't take the criminals long to discover that there were two Jim Strong's about that night. One of them, obviously would be stamped an impostor and that one would be the Major. Afterward, his chances of living would be even slimmer than they were in the beginning, which would be very, very slim indeed.

Jackson's problem was as straightforward as it was difficult. Should he abandon his ordered post here, attempting to free the real Jim Strong before the false Jim Strong's identity could be questioned—or should he stand by in the apartment to receive any messages from Nita and the Major, and to prevent a slip-up in the Major's alibi, should the Commissioner telephone?

"You will help me, won't you?" the girl asked again, a sob sounding in her voice with the desperation she felt.

Jackson's answer came slowly, reluctantly. "Wait until I get my automatic," he told her, "then just lead the way!"

The house Mary led Ronald Jackson to was one of those old-fashioned brown-stone homes on the upper west side of the city. A block away, the Hudson could be seen, but the setting only emphasized the fact that the street had long since seen its best days and was now grimly fighting for existence by taking in roomers and offering a policy of no-questions-asked in return for cash-on-the-line.

Jackson, unlike Ram Singh, believed that brute force could frequently be advantageously joined with deception and guile in attaining one's desired ends. He liked to do his planning first and his shooting, if necessary, afterward; the Sikh asked only a knife, a gun and a gang to confront him. This time, though, Jackson realized he'd have to adopt Ram Singh's strategy. There was no opportunity for planned deception—and there was no time for any fancy development of tactics. He had to complete this job quickly and—most important of all efficiently.

Leaving Mary Hicks in a drug store on the corner, he walked down to the house in the middle of the block. Its upper stories, he noted, were tightly shuttered and no signs advertised "rooms to let" in the lower windows. His gun held ready in his pocket, he climbed the weathered stoop and pressed the bell. When nothing happened after a minute's wait, he punched the bell again, this time holding the button down for long seconds as the pealing clangor shrilled imperatively within.

The bulky man who finally answered the door was red-faced and scowling. It was obvious he didn't like Jackson's approach—just as Jackson didn't like the way he held his right hand suspiciously in the side pocket of his coat. For a second or two the ex-soldier's level gaze held the other man's eyes.

"You did the ringing," the bulky man said finally in a deep, gratingly hoarse voice. "Now do the talking. What is it you seem to want so badly?"

"A room," Jackson told him on the spur of the moment, ad libbing as he went. "What are your rates?"

"You see any sign in the window?" the big man demanded, still blocking the doorway with his solid body. "When you see one, we'll have accommodations. Until then, this is a private house."

"That's fine!" Jackson told him, smiling. "I'll have a look at what you've got vacant. You see, I was anxious to locate here. The joint was highly recommended by a close friend of mine."

Instead of blowing up, as he'd apparently been on the verge of doing, the gorilla showed a certain puzzled interest at the mention of "a friend of mine."

"What's this pal of yours know about this place?" he asked now. "What would his name be?"

"His name's Colt!" Jackson snapped, jamming his gun into the big man's paunch and stepping quickly to the side and away from the other's concealed gun. "Do I get in, Fatso or do I shoot in?"

Surprisingly, the thug smiled, showing a stubby row of broken teeth. "You want in that badly," he said, "you get in. Could be, though, you'll want out even worse. Come on, sucker!"

Jackson wasn't playing this ahead; he was calling the cards as they fell and he knew it was the dangerous game. There was no turning back now, however. Every sense alert, he pressed forward as the bulky man retreated, never allowing an inch of space between the other's stomach and the muzzle of his gun.

"This is trespass with force," the thug said now, his voice sounding troubled. "Technically breaking and entering. I could burn you down and the police wouldn't call it murder."

"Sure," Jackson said easily, smiling without humor. "Sure you could—if you were fast enough. Otherwise you might wind up dead yourself, Fatso."

The interior of the house was dim, twilight having set in already. After Ronald Jackson had reached cautiously into the thug's pocket and relieved him of his gun, he ordered the man to turn on a table lamp. It's illumination didn't help much, however; deep shadows bulked large in the corners of the high-ceilinged room. In all the house not a sound could be heard.

"Are you alone here?" Jackson demanded.

"Sure," the thug told him, warily measuring Jackson with his small red-rimmed eyes. "I told you this was a private home."

"We'll take a look." A troubled sense of something having gone wrong swept over Jackson. He hoped the girl hadn't been mistaken in identifying the house. ''Let's try the upstairs

first—up where the rooms are shuttered off. I have a hunch I might come across a friend of mine up there."

The bulky man shrugged, turned sloppily and started for the stairs, Jackson directly behind. On the next floor, prodded by Jackson's gun, they went to the front of the house and began working back down the hall. As they came to each room, the thug was ordered to throw open the door, switch on the lights and then stand aside as Ronald Jackson examined the interior. The oppressive silence, but for their shuffling feet and the creaking of the floor boards, plus the thug's willing obedience stirred Jackson again with uneasiness. Something was wrong.

"Look,'" the bulky man said at last. "You got me covered, so there's nothing I can do about it. But why all this search business? You say you're looking for a pal here. Okay, we are holding a guy. You'd find him sooner or later, I guess, so I'll show you the room. It's at the rear of the house, but the door is locked and there isn't any key around now. You'll never get inside."

"Get going. Let's see that room," Jackson ordered. And, when they'd finally stopped before a rear-hall door, he added, "Okay, Fatso, you got yourself a little job. Break it down."

"Now, look—" the thug began.

"Bust it down!" Jackson snapped. "And fast!"

The big man raised a ponderous leg, lashed his heel forward to crash against the handle, kicked again and splintered a panel. Three more pile-driving kicks and the lock gave; the door inched inward slowly and Jackson saw young Strong sitting on a bed, his arms roped behind him, his feet tied securely.

Perhaps it was the sudden sense of victory; maybe it has the deceptive obedience of the heavy thug, disarmed and under the muzzle of Jackson's gun—anyway, he wasn't prepared for what followed. The sweep of action caught him momentarily flat-footed and with his guard down.

Pretending to start forward, the bulky man suddenly threw himself backward with surprising agility. But Jackson, lithe and quick to respond, leaped backward too—and crashed directly into a strong pair of outstretched arms that clamped about him, imprisoning his gun hand at his side. Nor did the burly thug stop after his first maneuver. He twisted quickly about to crouch on hands and knees at Jackson's feet—and then snapped upward to send his skull crashing

against the unprotected point of Jackson's chin, lashing a right and left into the helpless man's face as he did so! It was a murderous attack, vicious and swift.

Ronald Jackson fought against the dizzy sweep of unconsciousness, struggled feebly against the hold about his body. He knew then that others had crept down the hall to gang behind him, their approach covered by the crashing thunder of the thug's assault on the door. And the rest had followed quickly.

Again the thug—snarling viciously now with a bullying vindictiveness—sent brain-rocking hooks, right and left, against Jackson's jaw. Unconsciousness, red with pain, followed. But before he went completely under, Ronald Jackson felt an even greater pain than any physical hurt.

He had failed. He had deserted his post at Wentworth's penthouse apartment, disobeying orders, no matter how good his reasons. In the moment of the Major's greatest peril, the help of one whom he depended was lost to him. Jim Strong, and the Major's impersonation of Strong, would shortly be apparent to the villains. And now poor little Mary Hicks had been delivered into their hands too. Bitter blackness drowned further thought....

14

MOUNTING DISASTER

AN oppressive silence held Nita van Sloan and Ram Singh as they drove back to the apartment. The heavy thoughts, the living fears of each were better left unspoken. Somewhere in the city Richard Wentworth was abroad on the most daring and perilous adventure of his action-filled career. Somewhere in the future, Nita had always known, there was a final adventure awaiting Dick. Was this to prove to be the one? Ram Singh must have wondered the same thing too. Neither spoke because each loved Dick, if in a different way and perhaps neither wanted to trust his voice.

Back in the apartment at last, Nita threw the switch for the living room lights, looked quickly about the empty room. Then her eyes sought those of Ram Singh, trouble wrinkling her smooth brow. Ram Singh scowled.

"Jackson!" Nita called. "we're back!"

"Come out, little man," Ram Singh added in his booming voice. "Don't hide. It's only us."

But the forced humor in Ram Singh's words was obvious. When only silence greeted their shouts, the full-bearded Sikh and the slim-figured girl began a systematic search of the rooms, no longer calling to Jackson. Was he, perhaps, wounded and unconscious, the victim of a sudden attack? But the true answer, when they met again in the living room, was even more puzzling and dismaying.

"He's gone, Ram Singh!" Nita said unnecessarily. "He isn't in the apartment! But what could have called him away?"

A low growl sounded in the giant fighting-man's throat. "He maybe has answered a sudden call from the sahib, missie sahib," he suggested, his voice lacking conviction.

"Maybe," Nita van Sloan agreed—but her tone was equally filled with doubt. Both of them knew that Dick wouldn't have called Ronald Jackson to him. Hadn't he already refused their urgent pleas to be allowed to accompany him that night? Further, in his guise as Jim Strong, the presence of any one of the three of them would be a dangerous give-away. Some other assignment for Jackson, then? That was possible—but only vaguely so.

"No note," Ram Singh reported after scouting through the foyer hall where such messages were usually left. "He left no tell-tale writing for us."

"That can mean only one thing," Nita observed, her voice thoughtful. "He was called away on a desperately urgent mission. He didn't have time—or the danger was so great he didn't think to leave one."

"Could be Jackson expected the quick return," Ram Singh added. "Could be he'll appear momentarily."

Neither knew just which was the real answer—and both of them felt so helpless in their present position. Dick was gone, they knew not where. And now Ronald Jackson was missing from his post without a word of explanation.

To Ram Singh, the living embodiment of all the great warriors of the ages, this inactivity was especially painful. He swung on his heel now and left the room, walking out onto the dark terrace. There, under the stars and looking down majestically on the twinkling myriad lights of the city, he began to pace up and down. His giant strides, quick with his own seething impatience, told of his state of mind, his eagerness for action.

Now, in retrospect, he could recall the strange whistling sounds he'd heard as he'd stood in front of the dark East Side Bar.

They had been signals, he realized—but did they concern Richard Wentworth, his sahib? That he couldn't answer. But he was afraid, this huge man who knew no fear for himself.

Sitting quietly in the living room, Nita van Sloan tried to force her thoughts to other channels. She relaxed in an easy chair and pushed a button on the table at her elbow. Muted melody filled the room as four concealed loudspeakers whispered the strains of a symphony. But the music did no good.

Nita wondered again if that strangely familiar figure she had seen briefly on the sidewalk could have been Dick in his disguise. True, the man had turned into an apartment entrance almost immediately the Daimler had come into his sight. But wouldn't that have been just like Dick, if he were in the middle of a closing trap? Rather than accept the aid of those he loved, when possible failure would have meant death for them, he would have willingly accepted any personal disaster for himself.

Suddenly Nita turned off the soft music. Through the open doors to the terrace came the life-beat of New York City—those small night-sounds, thousands upon thousands from the teeming metropolis, blending into a whispered whole. A nameless, far-off something that was the living New York. A regular, heavier sound could be heard too: the stalking footfalls of the impatient Ram Singh as he paced his night-watch in the dark.

Somewhere out there, Nita knew, Richard Wentworth fought a gallant battle alone, and against impossible odds. Where was he now? How did he fare? And where was the inexplicably missing Ronald Jackson? Were they both still alive?

Suddenly Nita van Sloan's lips began to move faintly, without sound. She was whispering a prayer, simply and sincerely, for the man she loved with such a great love—and who loved her as well.

An excruciating pain jolted Ronald Jackson back to consciousness. He heard a voice shouting unintelligible words, then realized it was his own.

Slowly, as reason and awareness returned, he understood what it was that had been racking his entire nervous system. The pain had stopped now that his half-glazed eyes were open at last, but the soreness of the fingers of his right hand gave him the answer. Someone had been driving the blade of a small penknife under the fingernails of that hand, cutting into the sensitive nerve-centers there.

Still weak and dizzy, Jackson's head remained tilted forward, his chin resting on his breast. A hand seized his hair, snapped his head back and a near-blinding light blurred his vision. In the background he heard someone laugh, heard a chair scrape on an uncarpeted floor. The air of the room in which he found himself was pungent with the smell of a strong cigar.

With the passing seconds, Jackson's eyes became accustomed to the glare. Directly opposite him was a large desk and a fat man sat behind it, a cigar tilting out of one corner of his mouth and a derby hat perching on the back of his head. He was scowling at Jackson thoughtfully, the fingers of one pudgy hand beating a silent tattoo on the desk top.

Against the wall and to Jackson's left lounged the original thug he'd met at the door; to his right, seated in reverse on a straight-backed chair, his crossed arms leaning on the back, was a third gang member. This third man was thin almost to the point of emaciation and his rat-featured face spoke of his vicious cruelty. It was undoubtedly he who had been the knife-artist a moment before. A thin smile of satisfaction quirked his mouth.

"So you've come back to join the living for a little while," the man behind the desk said softly. "Maybe you don't like it so much after a while. Maybe you don't like it at all!"

The thin man laughed mirthlessly. "You want I should go to work on him now, boss? Just give him a little sample?"

The fat man waved his cigar in the direction of the voice, silencing the thin man without looking at him, then returned the cigar to his thick-lipped mouth.

"What do you know about this kid, Jim Strong?" he demanded next. "How come you're interested in him—and how come you knew you'd find him in this house?"

Jackson thought quickly, despite his throbbing head. This line of questioning was

getting close to the Major; next they'd want to know who he worked for. He had to watch his answers, make them plausible and at the same time misleading.

"I heard he was being held here," Jackson replied cautiously. "I came down to investigate, to find out why."

"You heard!" The interruption was contemptuous, angry, and for the first time the fat man allowed his voice to rise. "Listen, punk, you better answer my questions straight—and in detail. I'm telling you that for your own good—and for the last time. Now, then: just who told you— and how did they get that information? Talk, and talk fast!"

"A girl told me," Ronald Jackson said. "Her name is Mary Hicks. She's this guys sweetheart as well as a close friend of mine. She came to me to help her."

"Mary Hicks," the inquisitor repeated. "Okay. Now go on with the answers. How did she get the information?"

"She saw the whole thing happen," Jackson told him. "She was on her way to meet the guy when she saw him jumped by a gang and taken away in a car. She followed in a cab, checked the address and came directly to me."

The thin man began to swear, his face contorted. The sound of that made Jackson glad. It meant he was being believed—and he had little fear that the thugs could trace Mary Hicks back. She probably wouldn't wait too long at the drug store where he'd left her, before going to the police as a last resort. Now, if he could only delay the scheduled execution of the gang....

"Rot!" the fat man exploded. "that's a damned lie! As a story, it's okay; as the truth, it stinks! Maybe you need a little persuasion, after all! Okay, Soupbone, go to work on the punk— only don't let him pass out just yet."

The thin man came quickly to his feet, knocking the chair over as he did so. The bulky man who lounged against the wall straightened now, a sudden look of distaste coming over his face. He had evidently seen the emaciated thug "go to work" before and had no desire to watch the proceeding again.

Jackson realized the nature of his fate. "Just one moment," he said, his voice so controlled and unafraid that the others paid attention to him in spite of themselves. "Before you begin this nonsensical butchery, which will get you nowhere,

tell me one thing. In what way does my account of the facts sound so ridiculous?" If there was calm assurance in his tone, fear knotted his stomach and his palms were wet with sweat. Such characters as these weren't anything new to him, nor did he doubt the entire sincerity of their threats. He had been in such jams before.

For a moment the fat gang leader seemed undecided whether to reply; finally he condescended. "I just got a report, punk, that another group of the gang picked up a second Jim Strong tonight, down on the lower east side. My job now is to find out which is the right one— and which one is the phony!"

A shock of fear went through Ronald Jackson at those words. The Major had been trapped, caught! Now, with the real Jim Strong in their hands, the deception would be uncovered— and Richard

Wentworth would be revealed as the impostor! Afterward, of course, both men would suffer summary execution!

Jackson forced a laugh, an easy carefree laugh. "Someone's playing you for a bunch of suckers!" he said. "Maybe the real Jim Strong is still at large! I'll give you ten to one he is!"

His laugh, in addition to what he said, caused red fury to mount into the cheeks of the fat leader. He came slovenly to his feet, his hands gripping the desk.

"The works, Soupbone!" he snapped. "See if you can't cut some of the answers loose from this wise guy!"

15

THE CLOSING NET

RONALD JACKSON knew it was coming then—if only in pure vindictive revenge. He braced himself for the attack, knowing he'd go down fighting, no matter how impossible the odds. But he felt a little sick as he watched the emaciated man draw a long-bladed knife from a sheath, run a cautious finger along its razor-sharp edge, and then begin to advance warily, half crouching as he slowly circled the defenseless prisoner.

"If you change your mind about telling me the truth," the fat man said, "I'll give you an easy out. You can die under the slugs of your own gun." A solid thump on the desk top told Jackson that he had laid the gun out by way of emphasizing his words, leaving it in plain sight. "Otherwise—" he concluded—"the knife!"

Jackson didn't bother looking around; he kept his eyes on the circling figure and came slowly to his feet, knowing that even if by some miracle he did succeed in throwing his adversary, the other men would rush him from each side. Ronald Jackson didn't try to kid himself. This was the end.

Jackson didn't believe in miracles—but he almost did in that moment, for something very like one happened. The outside shutters on the two large windows at the far end of the room were suddenly wrenched noisily open—and two panes of glass shattered into a thousand flying shards immediately afterward. The room was under attack by forces come to aid Ronald Jackson!

The script for Jackson's death, written by the gangsters, went completely haywire then. Nor did Jackson stop to wonder who could have come to his rescue, since no one knew where he was.

Ronald Jackson's response to the crashing interruption was instinctive and almost immediate. He hurled his lithe body backward, smashing down on the desk with his hip and shoulder. One hand scooped up the automatic the fat leader had laid there, as the sheer force of his leap carried his spinning body across the smooth desk top to slam against the chest of the slow-moving man seated behind it. The two of them crashed to the floor behind, landing in a tangled heap.

The other two thugs, meantime, not knowing the forces that attacked them—and not being able to see from the lighted room out into the darkness beyond—immediately assumed that only superior forces would have made such an audacious attack. Their guns were in their hands instantly and panic caused them to throw shot after shot into the invisible beyond. Momentarily, they seemed to have forgotten the disarmed Jackson.

Jackson's first move was to pump two slugs into the chest of the fat gangster, mercilessly exterminating that many-times-over killer and his own intended executioner. The sound of the shots behind the two henchmen, however, reminded them of the danger in their rear.

The emaciated gangster was the first to react, whirling about with incredible speed. It was his last conscious move, though, for even as his revolver blasted lead at the desk-barricaded Jackson, the other's return shot shattered through the bridge of his nose and hurled him bodily against the wall. Without further sound or movement, he fell limply forward, collapsing in an inert, huddled heap.

Jackson didn't dare twist about to face the third thug; there wasn't time. No sooner had the last slug left his gun than he snapped his wrist upward, sending a bullet unerringly into the single large bulb that brilliantly illuminated the room. Darkness fell instantly like a blanket of blindness.

The ex-sergeant's next shot smashed into the wall in the exact spot in which the third gangster had stood—but a second later he knew he had missed. The door of the room banged open and racing feet could be heard on the stairs. He had seen his companions go down beneath Jackson's one-man barrage—though he probably thought others had aided the single-member riot squad—and he had no stomach for further battle.

Rising to his feet, Jackson heard someone jump into the room and a second later saw a match flare in the darkness. The match was joined by another near by—and two faces came into view. The first was that of Mary Hicks—and the second revealed Jim Strong's grim-lipped features!

"Jackson!" Mary called, her voice shaking with the shock of what she had just seen. "Jackson are you all right?"

Ronald Jackson's devil-may-care laugh greeted her question, showing his relief that the two kids were safe?" he repeated. "I'm spoiling for another chance at them!"

The house was deserted when they made their way quickly but cautiously downstairs. They all had as much to fear from the police as from such henchmen as they'd just fought. But the whole action had occupied only a chaotic minute or too, and luck was with them. They were stepping into a cab at the far corner as the first squad-car screamed up to the deserted house of death.

For the first half of the drive to the Wentworth home, little was said in the cab. Mary, in Jim's arms, would occasionally whisper something and he would reply in the same manner. As for Jackson, he sat well over on his own side of the seat, looking out of the window and whistling under his breath. His detachment somehow made the too young people feel almost alone. Much of what they had to say, however, needed no words to express.

Shortly before they arrived at their destination, Mary Hicks explained how she had waited in the drug store until she felt Jackson was overdue—and how she had then gone to the cheap rooming house next to the house he had entered. On the pretext of wanting a room and by actually engaging one—she had been left alone by the housekeeper. After that—showing a nerve that made both Jim and Jackson beam with pride—she had quietly mounted to the top of the building and gained the roof by way of a ladder and a skylight. But her problem only began there.

True, the brownstone houses on the block were identical in architecture and it was no great trick to gain the roof of the building in which Jim was a prisoner—and in which Ronald Jackson, evidently, was also trapped. But it was something else again for one young girl, unarmed, to hope to outwit a gang of thugs and release the two men.

It was Mary's nerve again—plus a stroke of luck, made possible by Jackson's earlier maneuver—that furthered the action now. She entered the criminals' hideout by the same method she had left the rooming house and crept cautiously down from the third floor to the second. And it was then she discovered Jim Strong, helplessly bound but revealed to anyone in the hallway because of the smashed door that sagged drunkenly on its hinges.

Released, Jim's presence gave Mary new hope. Perhaps, because of her love for Jim and her unbounded faith in him, she refused to recognize the ridiculously overwhelming odds against them. But the two of them agreed that any attempt to storm the door of the room in which Jackson was held would be futile and foolish. It was then they thought of the rear fire-escape that gave access to that room from behind.

Without any developed plan, they gained the two windows, armed only with improvised clubs wrenched from the shattered frame of the door inside. And the sight of Jackson's plight, spied through the slits of the shutters, made any further debate impossible. A diversion had to be provided immediately, for Ronald Jackson was on the point of being cut to ribbons!

The smashing of the shutters and the shattering of the window panes was the only possible following action—and it was exactly the diversion that Jackson sought. He had done the rest....

"Man alive!" Jim Strong laughed. "Now I know what the old time gunfighters meant when they called a man a shootin' fool!"

But Jackson was silent; there wasn't any laughter in him just then. He was remembering that Richard Wentworth's impersonation of Strong had been uncovered through the boy's seizure— and that Wentworth himself was now a prisoner in the criminals' hands!

It was but a block from the Wentworth home that Ronald Jackson's quick eyes spotted the dark sedan parked at the corner, five men seated silently within—and there was another at the next corner, undoubtedly others parked in the surrounding blocks! The gang was closing in!

Jackson jumped forward, slid open the glass partition behind the driver. "Keep going!" he ordered. "Don't pull up in front of the building! Pretend you aren't headed there!"

As they circled the block Jackson pulled a five-dollar bill from his wallet and handed it forward, giving the driver his instructions in short clipped sentences.

Then, as they approached the building again, one of the sedans behind them blared three quick notes on its horn—and another ahead answered immediately! The cab had been spotted!

But Jackson's plan was already under execution. As he turned the corner, the driver pulled close to the curb, cut his speed as though to coast up to the entrance—and as he did so, Mary, Jim and Jackson slid through the taxi's door and, crouching, ran to the covering darkness of the nearest building.

The intervening body of the cab had concealed their action from observation of the thugs. As they strode quickly toward the trademens' entrance to the building, they saw the taxi draw up in front. The uniformed doorman ran forward to open the door—and as he did so, dark forms rushed in from two sides. The doorman was knocked sprawling from a blackjack blow and the two doors of the cab were thrown open simultaneously—to reveal an empty interior. A second later the driver had released his clutch and the car leaped into violent motion, knocking the strong-arm thugs sprawling.

By that time, Jackson and his charges had reached the side entrance. As Mary and Jim disappeared into the basement hallway, he turned swiftly when a hoarse voice shouted close behind him. The roar of a gun came simultaneously with the thug's call, and whining lead whipped splinters of concrete stingingly into Ronald Jackson's face. The trio had been seen!

Jackson fired from his hip in that split-second emergency and the man went down as though pole-axed. Others were answering his call, however, and Jackson didn't wait for more. He raced after Jim and Mary, now well ahead.

For moments such as this, Richard Wentworth had a private, hidden elevator in the basement which went directly to his penthouse.

It was to this Jackson sped now. Behind them, their voices and running footsteps loud in the narrow concrete hall, they could hear their pursuers drawing close. But Jackson was ready. Sliding to a stop before a solid door, apparently one of the many storerooms, he slipped a key into the lock, herded Jim and Mary within. A moment later he had slammed the door behind him.

They were in a small, box-littered room: Just another store room, apparently. But at a touch of a button a whole tier of boxes in one section swung outward on silent hinges-and a self-service elevator was revealed behind....

Ram Singh was the first person to greet them when the door slid quietly open to admit them directly into the penthouse. The huge Sikh stood directly in the exit, blocking it completely with his massive body—and one large hand rested warily on the hilt of the long-bladed knife in his belt. Over his head a warning light gleamed redly, telling of the elevator being in use. It was always possible an enemy might discover this convenient access to the Wentworth stronghold.

Ram Singh's eager eyes told plainly that he had hoped he would see his sahib step jauntily into the room—but his joy was not entirely destroyed. A laugh boomed from his chest and he grabbed Ronald Jackson in his great arms, swinging him from the floor as though he were a child.

"Did I not say it?" he exulted. "This one always returns!"

Ronald Jackson's return had helped to soften Nita's disappointment, too. She came forward now to greet Jim Strong and to be introduced to Mary. Afterward, Jackson gave a recount of what had happened. It was as he told of the last episode, happening in the street outside, that Ram Singh jumped to his feet, a warning rumble sounding in his throat, and strode to the terrace outside.

Twice Ram Singh circled the terrace, and when he came back to the living room his face was dark with a forbidding anger and his great beard seemed to bristle defiance.

"It is so, missie sahib," he reported, his voice ominous. "The little men have surrounded us. These creatures have dared to assault the very home of the sahib! I shall go out and carve their foul carcasses! I shall crush their skulls like eggshells! If there are a hundred of them—"

"No, Ram Singh," Nita said slowly, quietly. We can only wait. The sahib must return soon!"

And Jackson swallowed painfully at her words. Delaying to the last his distasteful duty, he hadn't yet mentioned Richard Wentworth's reported capture. Now, as he told it, he didn't have the heart to look into Nita van Sloan's eyes.

"So there it is," he concluded tonelessly, his eyes still on the carpet and his ears actually ringing with the dead silence of despair that held the room. "The Majors held captive; we don't know where. And the gang's thrown a ring around the apartment—for an imminent attack; we can't tell when."

16

In Hell's Dungeon

RICHARD WENTWORTH relapsed into unconsciousness again after that brief period of half-consciousness in the automobile that sped him away from the scene of the fight near the East Side Bar. He had no way of telling, but not much time seemed to have elapsed before he came fully out of the coma.

Slowly the present came back to him, and with that aching return there came memory of the events that had led up to his mental blackout. But for long minutes he didn't move; he gathered his strength for the dangerous struggle that would soon came. Time was short; he knew that. Somewhere in the background, like a warning metronome of disaster, he could hear water dripping with the slow monotony of inexorably advancing time.

He was lying on a rough stone floor — apparently a dungeon-like basement, paved with uneven blocks. The floor was damp, too — a further indication that he was below street level.

About him the illumination was dim and flickering: probably gas light, Wentworth guessed. The sound of many feet shuffling in the background told him there were others present—probably all of them members of the criminal horde that had descended upon the city. There was but one answer to that. He was at the gang's headquarters!

What would have brought despair to any other man, only made Richard Wentworth grin in triumph. He had succeeded! He had achieved exactly what he had sought! As Jim Strong he had been seized and brought to the execution chamber! Nor did he wonder how he could bring disaster to these criminals, his brain and strength against that of many.

Richard Wentworth and the *Spider* never thought of the possibility of defeat, nor of its consequences. They had but one all important goal ever in mind: success! Nothing else could be given a moment's consideration.

After a time, Wentworth got to his feet, noting with satisfaction that except for the wound in his side, he had suffered no further severe wounds. Then his hands went to his face, his sensitive fingers quickly running over its contours, and he nodded with satisfaction. His disguise had remained undamaged; he was still undetectable as the young Jim Strong.

Next he examined the room in which he found himself. It was small—no larger than the average police cell—and its walls, floor and ceiling were composed of solid stone blocks. The only furniture in the windowless cell was a narrow wooden bench, and at one end stood a steel door with a small grillwork of bars, giving into the room beyond. Through the grill filtered the uncertain light that dimly lit the cell.

Richard Wentworth went to the door of the cell, gripped the steel bars with his hands and drew himself up from the floor until the aperture was at eye-level and he could peer out. A great expanse of cavernous room lay beyond, its space broken only by huge stone pillars that flared wide at the top to support the vaulted ceiling. Each pillar carried a brace of gas jets which lighted the place, as he had guessed. On the far side of the room he could see another tier of cells similar to his own, and he knew that the one in which he was imprisoned was part of a similar row.

At that moment one of the guards came into view. He was a typical underworld gorilla, even his long simian arms and waddling gait seeming to copy that of his animal counterpart. He carried a gun in a shoulder holster and a long club in his right hand, while a bunch of keys jangled on a ring at his belt.

At first he didn't notice Wentworth hanging from the bars, but then he caught sight of the fingers gripping there. With a grunt he changed his direction and slowly, casually approached the cell.

Suddenly—when he was about six feet away from the door and without the slightest warning— he leaped toward Wentworth and swung his club viciously at his exposed fingers! The murderous blow crashed against the steel bars but a second's fraction after Wentworth's superbly reacting muscles had snapped his fingers free and he had dropped to the floor. That sly, deliberate trick might have cost Wentworth the loss of several fingers! He stood in the semidarkness below and seethed with anger.

"Too bad, sonny!" the guard sneered. "In this place we don't tell you what isn't allowed—we show you, the hard way, the first time you do it! Now maybe you won't try that one again!"

His words and the harsh laugh that followed indicated that he thought he had succeeded in crushing his prisoner's hands and, with any other man, he would have succeeded, too.

"I have a little score to settle with you, my lad," Wentworth whispered to himself when the other had gone on his rounds. "And, since I don't have anything to do just at the moment, I think I'll settle that account right now!"

Wentworth's eyes swept the cell again but the wooden bench was the only tool or weapon he could discover. He considered its usefulness, knowing it had to be his means of escape—and within a few seconds had his entire plan! He grinned in the dark, the merry twinkle of a coming dangerous contest lighting his eye.

"And while I'm at it," he added to himself in a whisper, "I might just as well walk out of this cell! Frankly, I find it rather confining in here!"

In that moment's thought he had reasoned that the guards outside were unable to see into the cells because of the comparatively light place in which they walked. It was simply the sight of gripping fingers on the illuminated bars outside that gave a man away. So, Wentworth had decided to elevate himself to the ten-foot high grill without touching the bars—and then to overpower the guard silently through the bars, disarm him, and take his keys!

First he removed his belt, then he up-ended the six-foot bench, and finally climbed the vertical wooden seat to perch himself precariously on the upper legs. That done, he slipped the tongue of the belt through the buckle, fashioning an excellent leather noose thereby. After that, he waited silently.

The waddling guard appeared a minute later, passing directly under Wentworth's small "window" and immediately afterward was whipped from his feet as the coiling leather belt fell about his neck, was wrenched tight and tremendously powerful arms lifted him bodily into the air, dangling helplessly!

A short, strangled gurgle was the only sound he made. The club fell from his hand and he clutched and clawed at the garret that—was strangling out his life. His body twisted and swayed, his legs kicked a macabre dance in the air—but his movements slowly subsided, finally ceased entirely as his purple face fell toward his chest. He was unconscious.

In his cramped position, Wentworth was laboring under a terrific strain. The cords in his neck stood out prominently: sweat beaded his brow; his steel-siniewed muscles quivered under the enormous task; and his teeth were tight-clamped in effort. Every muscle in his body was aching in protest after a minute of supporting over two-hundred struggling pounds of weight!

The hardest part of the job was still to come, though, and it had to be done quickly, before the guard was missed or this action observed. To complete the maneuver, Wentworth quickly transferred his left hand from the belt to the man's neck, crooking his elbow around the throat. Next his right hand shot down to clamp itself under the armpit and across the chest, releasing the strap entirely. Then he used his left arm again, the hand gripping the other's belt and holding the limp form secure. A moment later he had the keys to the cell. A dull thud on the floor outside was the concluding sound of that near-silent battle: Wentworth had released his unconscious victim.

Seconds later Richard Wentworth was outside the cell. Free! Free, that is, of the cell—for between him and complete freedom stood thick stone walls and a small army of desperate men! But he was wearing the guards tattered cap, had appropriated his gun, and had locked the cell door on the thug.

There had been no need to gag the criminal. The fall must have done it. When Wentworth went to pick him up he had seen the impossible twist in the man's neck—and he knew he was dead. As dead as he and his companions had sworn Wentworth should be within a matter of minutes!

Wentworth had the guard's bunch of keys, but they were undoubtedly for locks of comparatively small importance, such as the cell doors. It would be foolish to hope that one of them would pass him—in to any chamber of major importance—or open a door leading to the outside and freedom.

On quick, silent feet, Richard Wentworth went to the nearest pillar and surveyed the great room. It was then his brow wrinkled with puzzlement and a sense of impending disaster swept over him. The entire place was deserted! Not a guard was to be seen, where formerly a dozen or more had covered their posts in different parts of the dungeon! At that moment a deafening voice boomed with laughter through a loudspeaker located somewhere in the room— and then addressed Wentworth directly!

"Very clever, Strong! Well done! I was amused, sitting here, to see if you could succeed—and enjoyed the thought of what would happen should you fail! Do you suppose for one moment, Strong, you could escape this place as easily as that? Do you think this is some common variety of underworld headquarters? If you do, James Strong, you are a fool!"

At that moment every gas lamp in the place flickered and went out! Stygian darkness cut everything from sight in an instant!

Richard Wentworth hadn't been prepared for that. He had been trying to locate the source of the voice—and had been wondering how anyone human could possibly see into every corner of that huge dungeon while apparently invisibly seated somewhere else! And with the abrupt blackout, racing feet pounded on the stone, the sounds converging on him from every side! Forty or fifty armed men were charging him at once! Blinding searchlights suddenly cut through the dark, centering on Richard Wentworth from every side, moving deftly with his every dodging motion!

The charging pack flooded in upon him and he went down under them—and then a very strange thing happened. Wentworth—whom even gangs of men didn't charge without casualties for many of them and bruises for all—didn't put up so much as a show of a fight! He went down, under the tackling, clutching arms and lay there docilely! And for the first time in his life!

"Now you're getting sensible, Strong!" the booming voice rang out. "You can't win—make up your mind to that! You were impossibly lost when you fell into our hands; your death is certain, so make it as easy as possible!

"All right, you men—bring him back to my office. He's about to enjoy his last interview though maybe the word 'enjoy' isn't well chosen. Drag him up here! Lively now!"

Hauled and pushed, his arms twisted painfully behind him Wentworth was roughed across the room and toward the far end.

On the way, one of the thugs deliberately clipped a short blow to his unprotected chin, but he gave no sign of having felt it. He was still acting the part of a completely defeated man.

His strategy was simple. For one thing, it was extremely dangerous for him that the master of the criminal octave had observed him strangling the guard. Such tactics weren't those of young Strong; he'd never have succeeded in such a superhuman task—and that fact might uncover Wentworth's impersonation. Unobserved—as he'd thought—he hadn't thought it ill-advised to go out of character for a moment, though it was something he rarely did.

And another fact had prompted his seeming capitulation. His very plan in becoming Jim Strong and inviting capture had been to get to the headquarters of the gang—and after that to find a way to meet the master criminal face to face. And now he was being dragged directly to him! Should he fight his own plan? Here was success, just as he'd envisioned it!

A solid steel door stood at one end of the dungeon and it was opened only after two men, one on either side of the door, within and without, had shot back bolts and unlatched two separate locks. Then, beyond, a narrow stone stairway round upward to the floor above. At the head of the stairs a second steel door stood, similar to the one below and beyond that door sat the criminal who was destroying a city!

A second later, Wentworth stood before him eye to eye....

17

CONDEMNED!

IMMEDIATELY after capture, of course, Wentworth had been disarmed. Now a strong pair of manacles were snapped about his wrists, locking his arms behind him, and a second pair— the chain between them no longer than twelve inches—was locked about his ankles. The man whose criminal empire had challenged a city certainly was not taking any personal chances!

The underworld leader was masked, of course. A black hood completely covered his head and neck, and he crouched behind his desk like a carrion bird sighting death. For a moment the two men faced each other in silence, and Richard Wentworth had time to observe the features of the room.

The walls were covered with thick, expensive velvet drapes but it was certain that thick stone backed them up. As for the rest of the furnishings, they were modern, tasteful and costly. That bespoke a man of intelligence and breeding—as had the voice Wentworth had heard on the loudspeaker.

Then, on the wall nearby, Wentworth saw the explanation for the hooded man's seeming supernatural omniscience for what went on in the cavernous chamber below. Neatly showing on a six by six foot screen, as in a moving picture, was a miniature picture of the entire dungeon, cells and all! But it was a picture that moved! It was an extremely clever television recording of the whole place! Even as he looked at it now, he saw two tiny figures make their way across the floor, open the door of the cell he'd quitted, and carry out the dead body of the vicious guard.

"You are soon to die, of course." the hooded man opened the conversation, his voice quiet and matter of fact. "I arranged this interview in order to ask certain questions. Ordinarily, condemned citizens aren't accorded such elaborate treatment—in fact, most of them never even see the inside of this headquarters. That is reserved for those who prove difficult."

"If I'm to die," Jim Strong's likeness asked, his voice as casually conversational as the hooded man's, "what makes you think I'll answer any questions? What have I to gain?"

"You'll answer them," the other told him, his voice ringing with confidence. "And you'll answer them gladly—to save others from a similar fate to yours. Your sister and parents, for instance. Or that girl you love!"

Fear ran through Richard Wentworth then, for how could he answer questions about which he knew nothing—make replies that only Jim Strong could know? And his fear was for the consequences which others could have to pay.

"I'll strike a bargain with you," Wentworth said. "I'll answer your questions to the best of my ability, if you'll tell me a few facts too!"

The sound of the hooded man's voice as he replied indicated that he was smiling. "I like you, Strong," was his surprising remark. "You've amazed me with your resourcefulness and your courage. I'll accept that bargain. And now, my first question: Why did you go to Richard Wentworth for help?"

"I didn't. My sister went for me—and I sent her because he is an old friend of the family and a famous criminologist. I knew he could help me."

"Next question: How much did you tell him? And why should you tell him rather than the police?"

"I avoided the police because they'd only have railroaded me—though unknowingly—for a crime I didn't commit. And I told Wentworth everything I knew which was no more than the public reports in the papers."

For the first time nervousness, apprehension crept into the masked man's voice. "I've observed," he said, "that whenever Richard Wentworth is engaged in a criminal investigation, the *Spider* also appears. The *Spider* has entered the present case. Now, as a friend of Wentworth's, have you learned whether he is a friend of this *Spider*? And do you think he would go to the *Spider* and report to him any inside information he may have gained—such information as he may have gained from you, without your seeing the importance behind something you told him?"

Richard Wentworth's Jim Strong had difficulty in restraining the smile that wanted to come to his lips. "I've never discussed the subject of the *Spider* with Mr. Wentworth," came the ingenuous reply. "It's a rather sore subject with him; he's touchy about it. You see, many people have held the same suspicion and have pestered him with questions. Especially Commissioner Kirkpatrick. But I will say this: it is my firmly convinced belief that Richard Wentworth and the *Spider* have never sat and discussed anything together! In fact, I'm sure they've never seen each other face to face!"

As the hooded man let out an almost imperceptible sigh of relief, Wentworth couldn't restrain one last barb. "And you asked me if I thought Richard Wentworth would go to the *Spider* with any private information. If you knew the *Spider*, you'd realize how ridiculous such a question sounds. The *Spider* needs to be told nothing—because everything is known to him!"

The hooded man glanced sharply at the Jim Strong before him, but his apparent nervousness restrained any remark. Instead, he seemed to be speaking to himself as much as anyone else. "I think we're about to close up shop for a while, until matters cool down a bit." His arm reached for a push-button on the desk. "which means, of course, that you've just heard your exit line, Strong—an exit right out of this life!"

"Wait!" There was no mistaking the urgency in Wentworth's tone. "The bargain we made! You said—"

"All right, but let's get it over with," the hooded man surprisingly agreed. "You've got exactly two minutes by my watch."

"First, why was I framed for the murder of my uncle?'"

"To save someone else from suspicion, obviously," the short answer came. "We needed a stooge."

"Then why am I slated to be killed now? Why not simply let me fight that frame—or even flee the country?"

The hooded man seemed to debate whether to answer; he glanced quickly at his watch, then let out a breath. "Okay, I'll give you the set-up, but briefly. First of all, I'm a businessman and my business is murder! I'm efficient at it. If anyone wants someone else rubbed out, they can come to me and I'll take care of it. For a substantial sum, of course."

"Just like that Murder, Inc. gang that's already been cleaned up!" Wentworth burst out.

"Not quite. You see, that was run by a bunch of butchers; they here bound to be caught in the end. My system had a new angle added—a fool proof angle. Once you've hired my men to kill someone off, the job is done. But—if any suspicion should happen to fall on you as a result—which means you might crack under

questioning by the police—I protect myself by the simple process of bumping you off too!"

The hooded man spread his large hands on the desk. "That goes for anyone connected with the crime who might have any knowledge that would lead the police to us: bystanders who observed the killing; the actual persons paying for the crime; even the gang member appointed to carry out the job. Your death warrant is signed once the police suspect you—and you possibly have the least knowledge pointing back to me.

"We try to protect our customers, of course; that's only smart business. For that reason, innocent persons are framed in order to throw the police off the trail. You happened to be one of those framed—to protect our customer, a man connected with your uncle's manufacturing firm who stood to gain thousands through his death. His name can't be mentioned, but it's in our files."

"But again I ask: why kill me? I know nothing of the crime!"

"Several reasons! the reply came sharply. "You went to see this Wentworth who's suspiciously close to the *Spider*; you knew about that dinner party, when your wine was drugged by a waiter to make you talk—wildly; you were eluding capture by the police, which did us no good; you had gained the confidence of your sister, who might conceivably turn your family in your favor—with their money and influence. In short, you were dangerous to me!"

The hooded man arose to his feet now, concluding the so-called interview. He reached again for the button, but before he could press it an urgent knocking sounded at the door— something that evidently was done only in extreme emergency. Quickly, the leader pressed a second button and the door clicked open.

The expression of alarm on the thug's face as he entered became blended with awe as he faced his master. It was obvious that this leader of criminals was as feared as he was mysterious. No more than five or six high lieutenants, probably, had ever seen his face or knew his identity. To the other hundreds of followers he remained unknown and apart.

Now, as the messenger whispered something in his master's ear, he came quickly to his feet and retreated to the extreme end of the room where the two held a hurried whispered conversation. To Wentworth it spelled but one thing: more trouble!

But during the moment he stood there alone, his mind was occupied with the knowledge he had just gained. What wouldn't the Commissioner have given to have learned it! No wonder there was no sensible connection between any of the wave of murders that had swept the city! How could there be—when this was simply a clearing house for mass murder!

Now he knew why that vicious gang leader had been so terrified the night he had visited the East Side Bar as Blinky McQuade; the man had evidently been one of these hired killers—and he had somehow bungled his kill, been spotted by the cops, and was then automatically slated for extinction by the master of the murder syndicate. From such an underworld conviction there was no appeal—and there was no hope of escape!

And Wentworth understood why "Big Bill" Dwyer had been summarily removed, too. As a politico-criminal contact for more commissions for murder he had slipped up when he'd telephoned the hooded leader to say Richard Wentworth had been in to question him.

Such a statement meant he was suspect— and it sealed his fate. That his death was also used to frame Nita, in the hope of controlling Wentworth's future actions thereby, was simply a spur-of-the moment by-product of his death utilized by the master brain.

Nor the pattern was crystal clear—but, for the first time, Richard Wentworth pondered if he hadn't paid too dearly to discover it. He wondered if his sands of time hadn't run too low for him to have an opportunity to make that knowledge known to anyone other than himself. He was still a fettered prisoner within one of the strongest criminal strongholds ever devised, and surrounded by a hundred vicious killers—their condemned victim!

Wentworth's thoughts came to an abrupt end as the two men at the far end of the room suddenly whirled to face him. There was something in their attitude—especially in the tense, half-crouch in which the masked leader held himself—that told him some further disaster had occurred. And when the leader spoke now, his words and inflection told plainly that the worst possible blow had befallen his already hopeless cause!

"James Strong," the bitterly sarcastic voice cut through the silence, "I have an astounding bit of news for you! There seems to be an identical twin of yours abroad—an identical twin who goes under the same name! One of you is a fraud— and may God have mercy on the masquerader who has tried to make a fool of me!"

A dozen rough hands seized Richard Wentworth before he could move, the strong-arm squad having rushed into the room as though by magic. But the secret signal and their sudden concerted charge hadn't really been necessary. Chained as he was, the impersonator of Jim Strong was practically helpless at that moment. But they held him as though he were the Devil himself—and the criminal master came striding across the room to face him.

"Bring me alcohol, ether and a wad of gauze," he snapped. "If this face is anything but real skin, we'll soon find out!"

He had hardly finished speaking before the requested articles were thrust into his hands. He dumped equal parts of each liquid onto the wad and began to scrub Wentworth's face. Nor did the prisoner offer any resistance; it would have been useless. As it was, the collodion, gum, greasepaint and gum Arabic that gave him the exact features of Jim Strong quickly dissolved. Within the space of seconds, as though by magic, a new, stronger set of features was revealed. A gasp went up from the assembled gang, superstitious fear evidently gripping some of them. Even the masked leader retreated two steps when the transformation was complete, his eyes gleaming brightly behind the slitted mask.

"Wentworth!" he gasped. "'Richard Wentworth. You here?"

Tight silence held the room for the following seconds. No one moved or spoke. Richard Wentworth himself knew that the ultimate misfortune had fallen—but he didn't flinch. He stood before them as straight and soldierly as a superior officer before his men—as commandingly as he'd stood, a Major, before his men in France. But what a different crew he faced now!

"Wentworth!" the hooded leader said again, but this time there was a vindictive triumph mingling in his tone. Then, as the restless movement of his henchmen indicated their anxiety for his command to make the kill, his voice cracked in command: "Wait! I have another idea! A stroke of genius!"

The seconds dragged by after that. Wentworth shuddered to think what could appeal more to this murderous madman than his own death—but he couldn't possibly guess the incredible evil that was churning in the man's twisted brain. A full two minutes must have passed before the underworld master spoke again.

"It's perfect!" he announced triumphantly. "There isn't a flaw or a possible slip-up!"

The gloating satisfaction in his tone made Wentworth's blood chill. Several of the gangsters in the background shuffled nervously as their leader paused in his dramatic announcement.

"My dear Wentworth," he went on at last, "tonight you are going to murder your closest friends! First: Nita van Sloan! Next: that barbarian, Ram Singh! After that: Jackson! Mary Hicks! And, perhaps, the Police Commissioner himself, should he happen to call at your modest penthouse!"

Richard thought the man was mad—until he heard the scheme. It was then that his heart almost stopped beating—because the plan of this genius of murder could succeed! It wasn't elaborate—and it betrayed his loved ones through their one great weakness: their return affection for Wentworth himself!

"You will be held here," the hooded man continued, "a prisoner for the next hour or two— until my plan is complete. In the meantime, I will go to your apartment armed with the very reason you have used against me! I shall go disguised as you, Richard Wentworth, their beloved master!"

He paused a second, seemingly breathless with the scope of his scheme. "The difficulties I have already disposed of. For instance, my method of entrance. I happen to know that you have a secret elevator giving access directly to your private quarters. Secret? There is no such thing where a clever man is concerned! I'll find it, you may depend on that! And when I step from that elevator, gun in hand, and in your perfect likeness—when your friends come rushing to greet me with joy in their hearts—what do you suppose will happen to them then? Just what will happen then, Wentworth?"

His last words had been practically a scream, and now he paused again, panting for breath. Afterward, he continued, "the police will be informed of your resolution. They will be told that you have suddenly realized how deeply you are involved in this crime wave that has been going on—and that, half crazy, you have decided to remove all trace of guilt by killing off those who have the knowledge that could convict you!

"The end, of course, will find you dead on one of the city's streets—perhaps the victim of a violent smash-up as you drove your car recklessly to escape pursuit.

"When that happens, the menace of Richard Wentworth's meddling will be removed forever! Men, take him away! Back to the cell!"

18

Is the Spider Dead?

BACK in Richard Wentworth's Penthouse apartment it was an anxious, worried group that sat there silently. It was Ram Singh who did the only moving about, made the rare observations on their position. Every five minutes or so he would go to the outer terrace and reconnoiter, and each time he returned, his face seemed grimmer than the last. As Wentworth's chief lieutenant of warfare, he seemed to have taken upon himself the responsibility of the group's safety until his master's return.

Mary and Jim, despite their present predicament, couldn't conceal the happiness they found in each other's company, no matter what the other circumstances. Ronald Jackson, characteristically, sat and oiled his Army issue Colt .45, quietly awaiting the coming battle— as he had done so often in France during the last war, Just before the zero hour of attack. Only Ram Singh stalked about, rumbling ominously in his beard.

"Missie sahib," he said after his last trip to the terrace. "These little creatures who skulk in the night are gathering closer! The power of my eyes in the darkness tells me they are also gaining the rooftops that surround us. Rifles, perhaps? Wah! What a way for men to fight! But, nonetheless, I would respectfully suggest we conceal the lights, make darkness our ally!"

Nita, who had seemed to have no interest in their present calamity—who seemed to be thinking only of Dick Wentworth—now nodded in agreement. "As you say, Ram Singh," she consented.

The men in the besieged group went about the room now, extinguishing the many soft lights that illuminated the large and handsome room. It was when they had all but completed their task that the first action came. A small window in one of the terrace doors suddenly flew into fragments, as though by magic, and a splintering thud told of a bullet embedding itself in the oak paneling at the rear of the room. The criminals were using silenced rifles that couldn't be heard in the street or in the surrounding apartments!

Muttering angrily because he was unable to come to physical grips with the whole criminal band, Ram Singh now ordered the girls in the group to sit in a far corner of the room where they would be protected by the wainscoting from stray bullets. Then he left the group momentarily, to return with a high-powered hunting rifle that belonged to his sahib.

Ram Singh walked onto the terrace, contemptuous of his physical exposure to danger, and threw the bulky gun up to his shoulder. The telescopic sight was silhouetted steadily for a second against the moonlight and then the thunderous roar of the big weapon shook the night. A mournful, eerie whining told of the super-speed bullet's flight and that wailing made by the steel-jacketed lead suddenly was drowned in a far-off scream. A human scream. And Ram Singh's booming laugh followed joyfully.

"Over the edge and down into the canyon!" he exulted. "Like a little clay pigeon on a wall! Happy landings, little man!"

Several times more Ram Singh shot—each time with telling effect; each time executing a short dance of triumph as he laughed in victory. But, after a while, the massive Sikh began to mutter and grumble once again.

"I like it not, missie sahib!" he declared at last. "My attack was good—but not that good! And yet they have retreated! There is none left to be seen! Who has ordered them away—and for what purpose?"

It was true. No more shots came into the room; no criminals could be spotted on the surrounding rooftops, though many others still remained on guard in the streets below. Some new attack was about to be executed; that much was obvious.

It was Nita van Sloan who saw it first— probably because she had been watching for it, praying for it all evening. Her glad cry aroused the others at once.

"Jackson! Ram Singh! Look—the light! He's coming!"

Just above the secret elevator door the red light glowered, telling of someone on the way up. It could only be Richard Wentworth, since all the others were here! Dick—the sahib, the Major had returned at last!

Nita was closest the door when it opened and Richard Wentworth stepped out. The glad cries of them all blended into one welcome. Nita ran forward to throw herself into his arms, her face beaming with a proud happiness. But she suddenly faltered to a stop, the joyous smile freezing on her lips. Her eyes were no longer on the familiar features before her.

Nita van Sloan was gazing in horror at the heavy automatic this strange Richard Wentworth carried in his right hand, leveled at her waist! And she realized with a sinking feeling that the others in the room couldn't know their awful mistake yet!

Thrown back into his cell, Richard Wentworth actually shook with the dread crisis that faced him. Because of what he had done, because he had allowed himself to be seized by the criminals, he had risked eventual detection. And, in that detection, he had given the master criminal the very weapon to murder in cold blood the very ones he loved most in this world! Now he swore— with Heaven's help—he would prevent such a dreadful tragedy!

In his own character now and no longer restricted by the personality of young Jim Strong, he managed to remove the flat leather wallet from his hip pocket. With the thin steel instruments in that case he quickly removed the manacles from his wrists, unlocked the leg-irons from about his ankles. And the door to the cell took but a second longer to manipulate.

The faint squeaking of the steel hinges behind them was the only warning the two guards, standing outside, had of what was happening. They had scarcely begun to turn before two almost impossibly strong arms seized them, smashed their heads together to drop them into instant and complete unconsciousness.

Panting slightly with the force of his pent-up energies and churning emotions, Wentworth surveyed the large chamber. It was deserted now. And why not? No man on earth—not even Wentworth, as the *Spider*—could have picked the locks on those massive steel doors that led to the outside. Not when such doors contained two locks, in addition to bolts, and when one of those locks was concealed on the opposite side, behind two solid inches of the finest steel! That method was impossible.

His next thought was to mix an explosive and blast the hinges loose from their rock beds. But he had to reject that. Such a method would bring the whole criminal army upon him—to face him, perhaps a hundred strong, in a narrow underground corridor! That, too, was impossible.

But he had to think of something! Time was fast running out!

Then, upon the heels of the thought of explosives, came a desperate, almost suicidal plan! Instantly, without hesitation, he put it into execution. Racing from pillar to pillar, he turned off the brace of gas jets on each one and then turned the gas back on again! At last, with the whole stone cellar rapidly filling with violently explosive illuminating gas he deliberately left one brace of gas jets burning, to act as a fuse. Wentworth then raced back to the open cell he had just left. In its small confines, surrounded by stone walls and protected by a near-solid steel door, he had the best protection obtainable. Beyond that, he lay at full length upon the floor, his feet and hands braced against the opposite sides of the chamber. It was the best he could do. He prayed it would work!

A single explosion in any part of the dungeon would have brought rapid concentration of the criminals to surround and cut off that spot. But a general explosion—one that would probably stun them all, or kill them outright—could lead to panic and confusion. No single portion of the underground dungeon could be detected as the point of action—and, best of all, not a single one of those steel doors could withstand that earthshaking blast! Such a door has yet to be made by man!

Blackness suddenly swept over Richard Wentworth. He was duly aware of a cataclysmic thunder that clawed at the ear-drums, wrenched the brain; he felt vaguely the spasmodic upheaval of the earth itself. And then blackness, unconsciousness.

But he wasn't out long. In his braced position, he had been protected from the worst of the physical effects and a momentary mental blackout was to be expected. It wasn't more than a minute after the tremendous eruption that he staggered out into the cellar again, dizzy but rapidly coming around.

The scene of chaos that met his eyes was astounding! Not a pillar had been left standing; rock and plaster from the ceiling had spewed down atop the other debris; the floor itself was a rolling, twisted carpet; and every steel door— within sight had either been blown from its hinges, or stood crookedly open to its greatest width. The path to the outside was open!

Wentworth's race with time that night was heroic. It probably wasn't more than fifteen minutes later that he sped in a cab toward his apartment. The one delaying factor that he was counting on to delay the criminal impersonating himself was the finding of the secret elevator, by which alone he could hope to gain undisputed entrance to the apartment.

Suddenly, however, a new problem entered the scheme of things, wrecking his plans. He leaned forward, called to the driver to pull to the curb—and then jumped to the street. For his quick eyes had spotted the underworld figures that lounged about in the neighborhood and he had immediately guessed the answer. His apartment itself was under siege!

Standing in the shadows, Richard Wentworth was undecided for a moment. He knew there wasn't the slightest chance of getting through that circling ring without being discovered. And yet he had to get through to save the lives of his friends! There was no other way it could be done!

But wasn't there another way? There was! As the *Spider* he could gain access to the penthouse—even if every criminal on the continent tried to bar his way!

One of Wentworth's many small apartments was located near by. Be sped to it now, and within the space of minutes the *Spider* stalked the streets of New York, his gliding black-cloaked form almost invisible in the night—but, had there been anyone to see, his face a horror to look upon!

The *Spider* knew his troubles were far from over. In such garb, he didn't dare risk being seen entering the building—or especially being seen near the private elevator to his home. Too often Kirkpatrick had set men to watch for just such a lucky break as that!

His final scheme was desperate, as it had to be. The ultramodern apartment building that stood next to his own equally fine place was almost as tall. From the roof there he might find a way of gaining his penthouse—but buildings such as these didn't have convenient fire-escapes on the outside for unobserved entrances. They did have, however, terraced apartments from the fourth floor upward, with their small outdoor walks in front of each—and the *Spider* asked no more.

The silken web laced upward two and three floors at a time, twining secure on the upper balustrade, and afterward the dark form of the *Spider* swung freely into space, worked swiftly upward. Ten or twelve such throws and he had gained the promenade roof, used in the daytime as a solarium for the tenants.

But he was still a floor below his own penthouse—and he couldn't just swing across space, and upward, at the same time! The solution to that was found a moment later. With the agility of a circus rope-worker, the *Spider* ran up the tall flagpole, held firm at the summit of the swaying wooden staff.

Out and downward the silken web snaked, to twine about the ornamental superstructure above his own apartment—and a second afterward the *Spider* swung out into space, the street twenty-odd stories below!

The arc of the *Spider*'s swing carried him over the outside terrace and directly up to the large French doors that gave out onto it—but he didn't try to check the hurtling force of his swing! Bodily he crashed through the doors, sending them slamming inward, and then released the web to sail on and into the room! As lithe as a cat, the dread form of the *Spider* landed in the center of the living room! So silent and abrupt had been his appearance that the others present at first didn't know he was there!

The underworld master, perfectly disguised as Richard Wentworth, was the momentary center of attraction! Automatic in hand, he stood before Nita, Ram Singh, Jackson and the two youngsters, Jim and Mary. So perfect was his disguise that in that dim light all but Nita looked at him in bewildered disbelief. She alone knew he wasn't the real Richard Wentworth because between Dick and she there existed such a perfect spiritual union that any deception was impossible.

As for Wentworth's impersonator, drunk now with the perfect working of his plan, he rocked back on his heels and howled with insane laughter. He knew that none of them would have dared use a weapon against him—with the exception of the knowing Nita—and he alone held a gun at that moment!

"Mr. Wentworth," the *Spider*'s soft voice broke in, "as one of your guests, aren't you ignoring me? Why don't you ask me to join your little party too?"

Wentworth whirled at the sound of that voice. The wild laughter became a choking gurgle in his throat, died away miserably. Livid fear blanched his cheeks and he took a step backward.

"You!" he gasped. Then, in a scream: "The *Spider*!"

"Yes," the answer came softly. "The avenging *Spider*!"

Only Nita van Sloan's eyes beamed with loving pride now. The others—Jackson and Ram Singh—looked on in blank-faced astonishment. It couldn't be possible! The *Spider* challenging Richard Wentworth to a death-fight—*when they were both one and the same person!*

19

THE SPIDER IS DEAD!

ITH a quick glance to Nita, the *Spider* sent her his message, one she grasped immediately: let me do this alone; just keep the others away! Then he turned back to face "Wentworth."

A sudden panic of fear seized the man—a fear even greater than his original terror. In that moment, insanity seemed to have gripped him. His arm flashed up to point the violently trembling gun at the *Spider*.

"Die, damn you!" he howled and fired as he did so!

But the slug hit nothing living. Almost as though by magic, the *Spider* was six feet away, a quick sideways leap carrying him easily from the bullet's path.

"Try again, Wentworth!" the *Spider* invited.

He was actually taunting Wentworth— offering his living body as a target! Unarmed, he was defying this madman to shoot him down! Screaming with rage, "Wentworth" shot again— then three times in quick succession. But each time that crouching figure with his belling cape was feet away from the path of the shot. The last two shots from "Wentworth's" gun where no more accurate; less so in fact, for his superstitious, trembling fear had increased as this seemingly bullet-proof apparition continued to stand before him unharmed.

"Wentworth's" last act was to hurl the heavy gun at the *Spider*'s head—and the other caught it easily, laid it aside on the table. The two men stood face to face—and, strangely, it was only then that "Wentworth" seemed to get control of himself. Perhaps it was the knowledge that life or death depended on his actions in the next few minutes, perhaps it was a supreme effort at self-control. No matter what, he succeeded.

"The last act, Wentworth," the *Spider* said. "The big scene—you against me—so let's make it good!"

The two men began to circle each other warily, arms held slightly out from the sides, eyes watchfully alert, and stepping lightly on tip-toe. Then, with the desperate savagery of a tiger at bay, "Wentworth" screamed a curse and charged ferociously, hurling himself straight at the *Spider*!

The bodies of the two men smashed together with the heavy sound of a great boulder smashing into a sandbank—and it was the *Spider* who gave ground! The charging head and shoulder of the powerful "Wentworth" had caught the *Spider* directly in his wounded side, re-opening that bandaged spot and sending liquid fire through his every fiber! In spite of himself, a gasp of pain was wrung from his tight lips.

That momentary advantage was all the other asked. A second lost to the paralyzing fire of pain can mean death in such a struggle! Now, by the time the *Spider* had wrenched his nerves and muscles back into coordinated play, "Wentworth" had managed to seize a small table and was swinging it murderously at his head! And the *Spider* was off-balance!

In order to avoid the blow, the *Spider* had to stumble clumsily to one side—and that again played into the other man's hands—for he was an expert in dirty rough-and-tumble tactics, a past-master of the lowest street fighting. With a bound he was upon the *Spider* and managed to twist his left arm up into the hollow of his back in a murderous hammer hold!

As this happened, Jackson gave a feeble, half-hearted cheer—and Ram Singh rumbled with uncertain disappointment. Then the too looked at each other in additional puzzlement. Neither could make up his mind yet which was the true master—Jackson thinking, perhaps that

"Wentworth's" pretended fear and panic was part of a strategy. Only Nita watched the *Spider*'s present desperate predicament with genuine dismay, her fists clenched tightly.

But "Wentworth's" hold didn't last long. With a sudden bound that carried him five feet up from the floor, the *Spider* managed to get his up-twisted arm down as low as his waistband then he turned in mid-air, and when he came down to the floor the two men stood face to face!

Stunned in turn by the sudden reversal of advantage, ''Wentworth" wasn't quick enough in the next action. His hand still gripped the *Spider*'s wrist—and now the *Spider* shot out his own hands, one to the others elbow, the other to his wrist. A lightening quick twist of his body, a mighty heave—and "Wentworth" was sailing through the air! He crashed into the opposite wall with terrific force and fell heavily, motionlessly to the floor.

For a moment the *Spider* stood where he was, one hand pressed across his eyes, the other supporting him against a table, and the mighty effort, plus his painful wound, caused him to sway slightly on his feet.

But he couldn't pass out now!

There was still too much to be done! Danger still threatened them all!

Now both Ram Singh and Ronald Jackson knew who the real Richard Wentworth was. If that last magnificent show hadn't convinced them, Nita's flurrying rush to be at Dick's side would help settled the matter. And, as Ram Singh went out again to the outer terraces Dick whispered to Nita, asking her to get Jim and

Mary out of the room for a moment on some diplomatic pretext. Although neither of them had watched the fight for more than a moment, it was best that "Wentworth's" true features be restored and the *Spider* meantime disappear.

As Nita complied with Dick's request, Ram Singh came rushing back into the room, his expression anxious.

"Sahib!" he exploded. "The Commissioner! I just saw his big car pull up in front of the house! He comes here!"

Commissioner Kirkpatrick on the way up— with both youngsters in the next room able to swear they had seen the *Spider* in that apartment, fighting with and killing the man on the floor! Kirkpatrick would know in a moment the *Spider* was Richard Wentworth— because no one had left the apartment in the meantime!

On the spur of the moment, Wentworth tore off the *Spider*'s garb, wiped his face clean of make-up and snapped orders to Ram Singh and Jackson. While Jackson removed the "Wentworth" disguise and substituted that of the *Spider* on the face of the dead man, Ram Singh dressed the corpse in the other garments.

And a moment later Commissioner Stanley Kirkpatrick strode into the room, his face grim.

"What's all this nonsense I hear, Dick, about your crazy talk of killing off—" and then he saw the dead ''*Spider*'' on the floor! He whistled softly and stood where he was, stunned.

"Kirk, you've been listening to anonymous telephone calls again," Wentworth chided in his usual bantering tone. Then, "oh, yes, we had a visitor. Most unpleasant sort of fellow. In the tussle I had with him—self-defense, you know— he seems to have wound up dead. Unfortunate! And, by the way, isn't he that *Spider* person who's been getting in your hair so often? I hope it's the same one, Kirk! I'd like to do anything to help you with that problem. It's annoyed me, too!"

Stanley Kirkpatrick was still staring at the body of the "*Spider*" when Mary happened to come back into the room. Her eyes popped wide when she saw Wentworth back on his feet again—for, as she thought, a moment before he'd been the one lying where the "*Spider*" was now—and the *Spider* had been the victorious one.

"Mr. Kirkpatrick!" she exclaimed, even though Jackson tried to head her off. "I thought you were—I'm so glad you're all right! That other horrible man—"

"I revived," Wentworth broke in hastily. "I managed to get up and finish him just after you left the room. Turned the tables, so to speak. Clever, eh?"

"What's all this?" Kirkpatrick asked suspiciously.

"Oh, yes, Commissioner!" Wentworth went on hurriedly. "That man confessed to this crime wave before he died—gave us the whole story of what's been going on, and why. Told me where we could find the complete files on all the crimes—files that would clear up every case on your blotter!"

The interest in Kirkpatrick's eyes was instant and intense; he had suffered much during the past days of horror that threatened the city his men policed and the citizens he loved.

"Why don't we take a run down to headquarters now while its still fresh in my mind?" Wentworth urged. Then, when he sat the Commissioner's eyes still on the grotesque form in the black cape and macabre make-up of the *Spider*, he added, "and, Commissioner, I'd better tell you—who was the real person behind this crime crave—as well as the person behind the *Spider*! It was that reformer fellow, Silas Breen!"

"BREEN!" Kirkpatrick burst out. "The man who suddenly got religion and sold out his vast manufacturing interests—which mysteriously collapsed shortly afterward!"

"The same," Wentworth said. Probably sold out because he knew the thing would collapse anyway. He only escaped investigation and indictment, you know, by the barest thread! And I suppose he figured out-and-out crime was a better paying proposition, anyway. Used this reform business simply to keep in contact with every branch of the underworld—and recruited his legions through those contacts. Rehabilitation, Incorporated thus became Slaughter, Incorporated! But I don't think you'll have much trouble wiping the whole business out once you've found those files I was told about."

When Richard Wentworth told Kirkpatrick he'd be with him just as soon as he got on his hat and coat, the gray-haired soldierly man didn't seem to hear him. When he returned a moment later, ready to leave for headquarters with Kirkpatrick, the Commissioner hadn't moved. He was still staring at the figure of the "*Spider*" lying so still on the floor. There were many emotions expressed in his eyes: puzzled wonder; the conflict of evidence and belief: hope that something will prove true which probably won't.

"It's incredible!" he was saying to himself. Incredible! I can't believe it! Yet..."

"Coming, Commissioner?" Richard Wentworth's suave, quiet voice asked politely. "We'll have a drink together after this business is over. How about it, Kirk? I think you owe me one for all those false suspicions you've had of me these many months!"

As the two men passed through the door, Richard Wentworth looked back and deliberately winked at Nita van Sloan. Ram Singh and Ronald Jackson grinned broadly as she winked back— and blew him a kiss.

Then the door closed behind them and the hard-heeled footsteps of the two men faded down the hall toward the elevator.

THE END

THE SPIDER WILL RETURN
in THE SHADOW OF EVIL
by C.J. Henderson
See next page!